"Fargo!"

Fargo's head jerked up as he heard the fear in the woman's voice.

A hundred yards away, three riders galloped toward her on sturdy ponies. They wore buckskins and feathers and war paint.

Some of Broken Hand's warriors had returned to the scene of the massacre, just as Victoria had feared.

Fargo never paused but kept running toward her. He bit back a curse. He was closer to Victoria than the Indians were, but they were mounted and he was not.

As he reached the edge of the pines, he lost sight of Victoria and the Indians. He ran through the trees, ducking low-hanging branches, guided by the shouts of the Crows and the screams that came from Victoria. As he burst into a clearing, he saw her running frantically toward him. The Indians were right behind her, about to ride her down.

Fargo fired on the run, a snap shot that flew true and caught one of the warriors in the chest. The heavy slug flipped him backward off his pony as if he had run into a wall.

MONTANA MASSACRE

by

Jon Sharpe

A SIGNET BOOK

SIGNET
Published by New American Library, a division of
Penguin Group (USA) Inc., 375 Hudson Street,
New York, New York 10014, U.S.A.
Penguin Books Ltd, 80 Strand,
London WC2R 0RL, England
Penguin Books Australia Ltd, 250 Camberwell Road,
Camberwell, Victoria 3124, Australia
Penguin Books Canada Ltd, 10 Alcorn Avenue,
Toronto, Ontario, Canada M4V 3B2
Penguin Books (NZ), cnr Rosedale and Airborne Roads,
Albany, Auckland 1310, New Zealand

Penguin Books Ltd, Registered Offices:
80 Strand, London WC2R 0RL, England

First published by Signet, an imprint of New American Library,
a division of Penguin Group (USA) Inc.

First Printing, July 2004
10 9 8 7 6 5 4 3 2 1

The first chapter of this book originally appeared in *Nevada Nemesis,* the two hundred seventy-second volume in this series.

Printed in the United States of America

PUBLISHER'S NOTE
This is a work of fiction. Names, characters, places, and incidents either are the product of the author's imagination or are used fictitiously, and any resemblance to actual persons, living or dead, events, or locales is entirely coincidental.

The Trailsman

Beginnings . . . they bend the tree and they mark the man. Skye Fargo was born when he was eighteen. Terror was his midwife, vengeance his first cry. Killing spawned Skye Fargo, ruthless, cold-blooded murder. Out of the acrid smoke of gunpowder still hanging in the air, he rose, cried out a promise never forgotten.

The Trailsman they began to call him all across the West: searcher, scout, hunter, the man who could see where others only looked, his skills for hire but not his soul, the man who lived each day to the fullest, yet trailed each tomorrow. Skye Fargo, the Trailsman, the seeker who could take the wildness of a land and the wanting of a woman and make them his own.

The Montana Country, 1862—
Where winters can be harsh and dangerous,
but not as much as evil men.

1

The distant popping sound made Skye Fargo rein the big Ovaro stallion to a halt. He frowned, his lake-blue eyes narrowing.

That sound meant trouble, no doubt about it. The question was, would he keep riding toward it, or would he veer in a different direction to avoid it?

A faint smile tugged at Fargo's wide mouth in the midst of his close-cropped dark beard. There was also no doubt about the answer.

He heeled the stallion into a fast trot toward the source of the gunshots.

A cold wind blew off the Rocky Mountains in front of him, slicing like icy fingers through the fringed buckskins he wore. Fargo knew that winter was fast approaching; normally he would not have been up here in the high country at this time of year.

But a friend had asked him for help, and Fargo was not the sort of man to turn down such a request. He had stocked up with provisions at Fort Laramie and then headed northwest, into the vast, sprawling reaches of the Rocky Mountain country.

The way Washington moved the territorial lines around, it was sometimes difficult for a man to know exactly where he was, at least according to the official maps. But the people who lived up here called the place Montana, and that was good enough for Fargo. Maps didn't mean all that much, anyway, where he was concerned. Skye Fargo was a trailsman. He knew where he was, pretty much all the time.

He was on his way to an isolated Army outpost called Fort Newcomb. It had been established earlier in the year to help protect the hordes of wealth seekers who were on their way west to the goldfields in Idaho Territory. Not surprisingly, the Indians who lived in this part of the country didn't like the ever-increasing numbers of whites moving across their land.

The summons that brought Fargo here came from the fort's commander, Captain Thomas Landon. Fargo had known Landon for quite a while and had worked with him a couple of years earlier, when Fargo was doing some scouting for the Army down in New Mexico Territory.

Landon had not gone into detail in his letter about why he wanted Fargo to come to Fort Newcomb, but that didn't matter. Fargo was willing to ride up to the fort just because a friend had asked him to.

But now, unless he missed his guess, those shots he heard came from the vicinity of Fort Newcomb. And that meant he was riding into trouble.

Of course, that had never stopped him before. . . .

The Ovaro's ground-eating pace made the miles roll behind them. Here in the foothills, the terrain was definitely rugged but far from impassable. After a time, Fargo spotted a column of smoke climbing into the arching blue sky, which made him even more worried about what might have happened.

Down at Fort Laramie, he had heard rumors that a large band of Crow warriors under a chief known as Broken Hand had been raiding in this area. Supposedly they had wiped out several parties of gold seekers.

But with winter coming on, there weren't many

prospectors traveling through the mountains in Montana, and the wagon trains full of immigrants headed to Oregon wouldn't return until the spring. Broken Hand and his warriors would have a shortage of targets to attack.

So maybe they had turned their attention to the Army post, Fargo thought grimly.

The smoke grew thicker and blacker. Fargo knew from the way it looked that it had to come from burning buildings. He rode around a bare, rocky knob of ground and found himself at one end of a long valley. At the other end lay Fort Newcomb. And just as Fargo had suspected, that was where the smoke came from.

The wind blew toward him and carried with it faint yips and shouts. Fargo quickly drew back around the knob and looked for a place of concealment. He suspected that the war party was coming right at him. It probably numbered at least forty or fifty warriors, maybe more, and one man was no match against such odds. As much as he disliked avoiding a fight, sometimes that was the only course of action that made any sense.

He found a crevice in the side of the rocky knob and swung down from the saddle to lead the Ovaro into it. It gradually narrowed down from six feet wide at the entrance until the stone walls came together. Fargo turned the stallion around and backed the horse as far into the defile as they could go, which was about forty feet.

Then he drew his Henry rifle from the saddle sheath and worked the lever to throw a cartridge into the chamber. He hoped the Indians would pass by without even glancing into the crevice, but if they spotted him, he would put up a fight. Only a couple of them could come at him at a time.

Unless of course they decided to stand out there

and fire arrows through the opening until he was riddled. Maybe it wouldn't come to that, Fargo thought.

He heard horses coming. The swift rataplan of hoofbeats grew louder. A large party of riders swept out of the valley. Fargo brought the rifle to his shoulder and nestled his cheek against the smooth wood of the stock. He held his breath as the war party galloped on past his hiding place.

He didn't let it out until the Indians had moved on without noticing him and the Ovaro. He had caught only fleeting glimpses of them, just enough to know that his suspicions were correct. They were Crow, and he had no doubt that they were the band of marauders led by Broken Hand.

But they hadn't seen him, and so—for now at least—he was safe.

He couldn't say as much for those poor devils at Fort Newcomb.

Although he didn't think so, someone might still be alive inside the fort. He led the stallion out of the crevice and mounted up. The Indians were out of earshot now, so Fargo took the big black-and-white horse around the knob and toward the fort at a gallop.

Fort Newcomb was laid out on a shallow bench of ground at the head of the valley. Snow-capped peaks soared skyward behind the fort. It had been built in the square pattern that most frontier outposts adopted, with a parade ground in the center surrounded by the enlisted men's barracks, officers' quarters, post headquarters, dispensary, mess hall, barns and corrals, blacksmith's shop, armory, and storage buildings.

Several of those buildings had already burned to the ground. The others were still blazing; orange-red flames leaped high from them.

Bodies lay everywhere, their blue cavalry uniforms darkly stained with blood. Some of the troopers had been mutilated so badly that even Fargo's strong stomach rebelled a little. Others seemed untouched except for the arrows that stuck out of them like pins in a pincushion. A number of the soldiers had been shot—an indication that some of the Crow warriors had been armed with rifles.

A few horses had been killed as well, but most of them were gone, driven off by the raiders. Fargo rode slowly through the carnage that littered the parade ground, looking for any signs of life in the sprawled bodies. His face was set in hard, grim lines as he moved toward the headquarters building.

The Indians must have torched it last, because although flames licked out through the broken windows, the building was still mostly intact, with the walls standing and the roof in place. An American flag flew from a flagpole in front of the building. It snapped and popped in the cold wind.

A cluster of bodies on the porch in front of headquarters told Fargo where the soldiers had made their last stand. He dismounted about ten yards from the building and left the Ovaro there, reins dangling. As he hurried up to the porch, his keen eyes searched the pile of corpses, looking for Tom Landon.

Fargo's friend was there, lying facedown across the body of another officer. Landon's hair was iron-gray, the color somewhat premature since he was only in his thirties. Fargo grasped his shoulders and rolled him over. The broken-off shaft of an arrow protruded from Landon's throat, and blood had soaked the front of his tunic.

Fargo dragged Landon away from the burning building and then went back to retrieve the bodies of the other men. It would take him a long time to bury all the dead men, but he would do it if he could. Chances were that Broken Hand and his men would not be back here any time soon.

They had already done what they came to do.

The roof of the headquarters building was on fire now, the flames leaping high. Fargo figured it would collapse soon. He bent to grab the feet of the last corpse on the porch, then froze as he heard a faint but unmistakable cry from inside the building.

Somebody was alive in there.

Without hesitation, Fargo bounded to the door, which stood half-open. "Hello!" he shouted. "Hello in there! Where are you?"

There was no reply. He shouted again, trying to make himself heard over the roaring of the flames. This time, a weak voice called, "Here! Here!"

The heat slammed against Fargo's face and stole the air from his lungs. He dashed back to the Ovaro and yanked his canteen from the saddle. Using the water from it, he soaked his bandanna and tied it over his face so that the wet cloth draped his mouth and nose. Then he ran back to the porch and plunged through the door into the inferno.

Flames were all around him. They licked greedily at his hands and the part of his face that was exposed. The thick buckskins protected the rest of him, at least momentarily.

The pathetic voice had come from Captain Landon's office. Fargo whipped through the door and shouted, "Where are you?"

Smoke-wracked coughing from somewhere low down drew his attention. He looked at the floor and saw a trapdoor beside the captain's desk. It was open, and someone was struggling to climb out. Fargo bent and caught the figure under the arms. He pulled the person up from a hollowed-out place hidden under the floor.

Fargo turned, wrapping the survivor in his arms as he lunged toward the door. A blazing ceiling beam crashed down only a couple of feet to his left. He didn't shy away from it, which was good because another burning beam fell closely to his right a second later. Fargo kept going straight toward the outer door.

When he was close enough, he left his feet in a dive that carried him and the survivor through the opening onto the blood-stained planks of the porch just as the rest of the roof collapsed. Little pieces of flaming debris landed around and on top of them.

Fargo scrambled up and threw himself off the porch, taking the survivor with him. He rolled over and over on the ground, putting out any small fires that might have sprung up on their clothing.

He knew from the weight of the person he had rescued that it was either a woman or a child. As he blinked smoke-reddened eyes and looked over, he saw that the survivor was a woman. She wore a gray woolen dress and had long, dark brown hair worn in a single braid hanging down her back. She shuddered violently as coughing spasms went through her.

Fargo pushed himself upright and then lifted the woman to her feet. He led her over to the Ovaro. She staggered and stumbled, but his strong grip steadied her. He got the canteen again and held it to her mouth, tipping it up so that a little water ran into her mouth. She coughed and lost most of it, but Fargo kept on until he had trickled enough water down her throat to relieve some of her coughing.

Something had started to worry him. He said, "Was there anybody else in there with you?" There hadn't been time to check, and he hated to think what would have happened to anyone unlucky enough to have been caught in there when the roof collapsed.

Much to his relief, the woman shook her head. "N-no," she rasped in smoke-tortured tones. "Just me."

Fargo nodded. He ran his eyes over the woman's body, checking her for injuries. As far as he could tell, she was unharmed except for a few places on her hands and face where the flames had singed her.

She reached for the canteen again. Fargo gave it to her and let her drink as much as she wanted this time. When she finally lowered it, she rubbed her throat. It would be sore for a while, but Fargo doubted if any permanent damage had been done.

Then, as the woman looked around, she slowly lowered her hand and her eyes widened with horror. Almost everywhere she turned lay the body of a dead cavalryman.

Fargo saw her eyes roll up in their sockets until nothing but the whites showed, and he was ready to reach out with one hand and catch the canteen when she dropped it. His other arm went around her waist to keep her from falling. She sagged against him in a faint.

Carefully, Fargo lowered her to the ground. They were far enough away from the burning building that she ought to be safe. One man had been left on the porch when Fargo heard the woman cry out from inside the building. His body was somewhat charred now, but Fargo managed to reach it and pull it away. He ignored the sick feeling in his stomach from the stench of burning flesh.

Fort Newcomb had been wiped out, the men posted here all massacred. Fargo needed only the evidence of his own eyes to know that. But the woman might be able to give him some details about what, if anything, had led up to the attack. Broken Hand must have attacked out of the blue, with little or no warning.

And when the woman got to feeling a little better, she could help him dig, too.

He went back over to her and saw that she had begun to stir. Kneeling beside her, he waited for her eyes to open.

When they did, she gasped and then started to scream and bolt up into a sitting position. Fargo caught hold of her shoulders and held them firmly. "It's all right," he told her. "You're safe now. It's all right."

Slowly, his words began to penetrate her stunned and violated brain. Her face crumpled into tears. Fargo pulled her against him and held her as she shuddered and wailed out her fear and anguish.

Finally she quieted, still sniffling a little as she pressed her face against his shoulder. Fargo patted her on the back, almost as if she were an infant in need of comforting.

"Are . . . are you sure they're gone?" she asked at last.

Fargo knew she meant the Crow raiders. "They're gone," he told her. "They rode off a while ago. I saw them leaving."

"But . . . they could come back . . . ?"

"They could," Fargo admitted. It was difficult to predict what a warrior on the killing trail might do.

She moved back a little from him, but kept her eyes on his face. He supposed she wanted to make sure she didn't accidentally see the evidence of butchery all around them.

"We should get out of here," she said.

Fargo nodded. "I thought I would bury these men first."

"There are . . . there are more than sixty of them. It would take a long time. And the Indians might come back. You said so."

Fargo couldn't argue with that. But he also couldn't stop a slight frown from appearing on his face. The woman was fairly young, probably in her mid-twenties. That meant she had probably been married to one of the officers stationed at Fort Newcomb. Yet she was willing to go off and leave her husband unburied.

He shouldn't judge her, Fargo told himself. Terror

had a way of keeping people from thinking straight. If they were scared enough, they would say and do things they never would otherwise.

Or maybe she was just the pragmatic sort. There was a good chance she was right to think that they would be safer away from here.

Fargo got to his feet and helped her to stand. "Tell you what," he said. "You take my horse and go down the hill to those trees. Keep a watch back down the valley. If you see anybody coming, you can warn me. I'll get this done as fast as I can." He had already abandoned the idea of getting her to help him dig the graves.

"I don't know . . ."

"There's a Henry rifle in the sheath. Can you shoot?"

She nodded.

He pressed the Ovaro's reins into her hand, then took her hand and held it in his own while he rubbed the stallion's muzzle with it. If worse came to worst, the big horse would let her ride him now. He might not like it, but he would allow it.

"Go on," Fargo told her. "The sooner I get started, the sooner we get out of here."

She was still reluctant to tear her gaze away from him, but she did it. As she started to turn and walk away, she paused and asked, "What's your name?"

"Skye Fargo."

"I'm Victoria. Victoria Landon."

Fargo's face didn't show the shock he felt. He knew good and well that Tom Landon couldn't have had a daughter as old as this woman, and he was pretty sure that Landon didn't have any sisters, either. That meant she must have been his wife.

So Tom Landon had gotten married in the two years since Fargo had seen him. Fargo hadn't heard anything about it. There wasn't any law against taking a wife, he thought as he went to look for a shovel. Nor was he surprised that Landon hadn't let him know about the marriage. He and Fargo had been friends, but they hadn't been that close.

And now that Fargo thought about it, he realized he shouldn't be surprised that it had been the captain's lady who was hidden in that hollow under the floor of the headquarters building. Landon must have put her there when the attack on the fort began. But why hadn't she come out earlier? Had she been so paralyzed by fear that she was willing to let the building burn down around her?

The questions could wait until later, Fargo told himself as he kicked a shovel out of the smoldering ruins of a storage building. The handle was charred and blackened, as was the blade, but the tool appeared to be in good enough shape that he could use it once it had cooled a little.

A glance at the sky told him it was approaching midafternoon. He wanted to put some distance between them and the fort before nightfall, so he couldn't take the time to dig a grave for each man. The best he could do was scrape out a shallow trench and pile the bodies in it.

The wolves would get them anyway, Fargo thought as he worked with the shovel. He couldn't dig deep enough or pile enough rocks on the mass grave to prevent that. So why was he even making the effort, he asked himself.

Because making the effort was one of the things that separated human beings from animals, he decided. The gesture might be futile, but it wasn't empty. It meant something.

"Fargo!" Victoria Landon cried.

Fargo's head jerked up as he heard the fear in the woman's voice. He tossed the shovel aside and broke into a run. When he reached the slope that led down to the stand of trees where she had taken the Ovaro, he saw her waving down the valley.

A hundred yards away, three riders galloped toward her on sturdy ponies. They wore buckskins and feathers and war paint.

Some of Broken Hand's warriors had returned to the scene of the massacre, just as Victoria had feared.

Fargo never paused but kept running toward her. He bit back a curse. He was closer to Victoria than the Indians were, but they were mounted and he was not. She shouldn't have let them get that close to her before she spotted them.

No time for recriminations now, Fargo thought. He drew his Colt.

The Crow raiders whooped and howled. Smoke plumed from the barrel of a rifle as one of them fired a wild shot toward the pines.

Fargo heard the Henry crack a couple of times. Victoria might be terrified, but at least she had the presence of mind to put up a show of resistance. The Indians' headlong charge slowed.

Fargo squeezed off a couple of shots from the Colt. The range was too far for the handgun to be effective, but the blast distracted the three Crows even more. One of them drew his pony to a sliding stop and lifted his rifle to take a potshot at Fargo.

Fargo heard the hum of the bullet as it passed to one side of him. He still didn't slow down. The other two Indians were closing in on Victoria. The Henry barked again from the trees.

As he reached the edge of the pines, he lost sight of Victoria and the Indians. He ran through the trees, ducking low-hanging branches, guided by the shouts of the Crows and the screams that came from Victoria. As he burst into a clearing, he saw her running frantically toward him. The Indians were right behind her, about to ride her down.

Fargo fired on the run, a snap shot that flew true and caught one of the warriors in the chest. The heavy slug flipped him backward off his pony as if he had run into a wall.

The other Crow swung his rifle at Victoria's head like a club, and only the fact that she tripped at that instant saved her from a crushed skull. The barrel of the rifle passed over her head as she fell. She rolled aside to avoid the slashing hooves of the pony.

Fargo leaped and tackled the Indian. The impact of the collision unseated the warrior and sent both men tumbling to the ground. Fargo landed hard. The Colt was jarred out of his hand.

But he still had the Arkansas toothpick in a sheath strapped to his leg. As he rolled over and came up in a crouch, he drew the long, heavy-bladed knife in one smooth motion.

The Crow had lost his rifle when he fell, but he yanked a tomahawk from his belt and lunged at Fargo, shouting defiantly as he charged. Fargo darted aside to avoid a sweeping slash of the tomahawk and swung the Toothpick in a thrust of his own that raked across the Indian's ribs.

The warrior yelled in pain and anger and came at Fargo again. The Trailsman dropped back and to the side and tripped his opponent as the Crow's momentum carried him forward. The Crow was too quick for Fargo to take advantage of the opportunity, however. He bounded back to his feet in the blink of an eye.

Fargo didn't know what had happened to Victoria or where the third warrior was, but he was well aware that if he took his attention off the man facing him, it could cost him his life. The Crow charged again, without any shout this time. The combat had now become a silent, deadly business.

But not completely silent. Steel rang on iron as Fargo's knife turned aside the tomahawk. Both men grunted occasionally with effort as they fought. Fargo went on the offensive, launching a flurry of slashing blows that made the Crow back off hurriedly. The man was stocky and strong, old enough to be a veteran of many horse-stealing raids and wars with other tribes. He fought well, and Fargo knew that an instant's lapse could be fatal.

Fargo had been in a lot of fights, too, and he was watching for his chance. When he pretended to stumble a little, the Crow's eyes flashed with anticipation of the kill. The warrior darted in, but Fargo was ready and went under the tomahawk. His knife came up so fast it was a blur. The razor-sharp blade sank deep in the Crow's body, ripping through vital organs.

Blood welled from the man's mouth in a bubbling sigh. His eyes widened and glazed in death. Fargo pulled the knife free and shoved the corpse away. It tumbled onto the blanket of pine needles under the trees.

Fargo looked around quickly, searching for Victoria and the third Indian. He spotted the woman sitting on the ground with her back against a tree trunk. She had the Henry rifle propped across her knees.

"I . . . I would have shot him," she said. "If you hadn't killed him, I was going to shoot him."

Fargo was glad she hadn't started blazing away at both of them while he and the Crow struggled. He sheathed the knife and then stepped over to her to take the rifle.

"Where's the other one?" he asked.

She shook her head. "I don't know."

Fargo spotted his revolver on the ground and snagged it, too, as he hurried to the edge of the trees. He saw the third Crow sitting on his pony about a hundred yards away. The man had pulled back while his two companions rode into the trees after Victoria.

The Indian had keen eyes, too. He saw Fargo at the

edge of the trees, pushed his rifle above his head in a gesture of defiance, and shouted angrily. Fargo whipped the Henry to his shoulder and fired, but the Indian had already jerked his pony around and kicked it into a run. The shot missed, and a second later the Crow disappeared over a small rise.

"Damn!" Fargo said.

"What's wrong?" Victoria asked as she came up beside him. "You scared him away, at least."

"He's not running away from me," Fargo said grimly. "He's running back to Broken Hand. And as soon as he catches up to the rest of that war party, they'll be coming after us."

2

The decision of whether or not to bury the victims of the massacre had been taken out of Fargo's hands. He and Victoria had to get away from Fort Newcomb as quickly as possible.

"Why did they come back?" Victoria asked. She shuddered as she looked at the two dead Crow raiders.

"No telling," Fargo replied with a shake of his head. "Maybe they decided they wanted to steal more from the corpses. What's important is that the one who got away will tell Broken Hand that someone survived the attack."

"But they killed everyone except me! Why can't this Broken Hand just let us go? Hasn't he done enough harm?"

Fargo smiled faintly. "That's not the way a war chief's mind works. He has to wipe out *all* of the enemy before he's satisfied. Besides, I killed two of his warriors. Now he has to come after me to satisfy his honor."

Victoria was pale with fear, but she nodded in understanding.

"Stay here with my horse," Fargo went on. "I'll see if I can catch one of those ponies."

The sturdy little horses didn't like the smell of him,

but he wore buckskins like their masters and he was able to approach them, speaking softly in the Crow tongue as he did so. Fargo knew more than a smattering of many Indian languages. As always, that knowledge came in handy. In just a few minutes, he was able to catch both ponies.

"You ride the Ovaro," Fargo told Victoria when he came back with the ponies. "He's pretty much a one-man horse, but he'll put up with you as long as I'm around."

She hesitated. "I've, uh, never ridden on a regular saddle before."

"Pull your dress up and throw a leg over," Fargo told her. "You'll manage just fine."

She did as he told her, revealing high boots and thick stockings as she mounted the stallion. Settling down into the saddle, she nodded and said, "It's not so bad."

Fargo swung up onto one of the ponies. The Crows rode with a pad and blanket, no saddle, but he didn't mind that. He was glad they hadn't been forced to ride double on the Ovaro.

Leading the other pony, he started down the valley and motioned for Victoria to follow him. "Where are we going?" she asked.

"When we get out of the valley, we'll see which way the war party went, and we'll go the other way," Fargo explained.

"Isn't there another fort anywhere around here?"

Fort Laramie was several hundred miles away to the southeast, but Fargo didn't mention that to her. To the north lay Fort Benton, closer than Fort Laramie but still a good distance away. Fargo was confident that they could reach either of the outposts, but the journey would take time and would be dangerous.

"We'll get back to civilization as soon as we can,"

Fargo said. "In the meantime, we'll be all right if we can avoid Broken Hand. There's plenty of water and game up here, so we won't go hungry or thirsty."

One more worry lurked in the back of his mind. At this time of year, a snowstorm could come roaring down out of Canada with little or no warning. Right now the weather was cold but clear, and the only snow in sight was on the peaks of the mountains. But that could change in a hurry. Fargo himself had run into such dangerous situations more than once.

Again, there was no point in talking about that to Victoria. He knew from the way she acted and talked that she had little experience on the frontier. If she thought too much about everything that *might* happen, she could grow paralyzed with worry.

Fargo kept his eyes open as they neared the rocky knob at the other end of the valley. He was almost certain the remaining Crow had hurried straight back to Broken Hand, but it was also possible that the warrior had decided to ambush them instead. As they rounded the knob, however, there was no sign of him.

The keen eyes of the Trailsman spotted the tracks left by the war party: They turned south. That settled it, then. Fargo and Victoria would go north and try to reach Fort Benton.

He pointed out the way they would go, then rode with Victoria for several hundred yards before calling a halt. "Stay here," he told her as he slipped down from the pony and handed her the reins.

"Where are you going?" she asked anxiously.

"To make our tracks a little harder to follow."

He walked back to the knob and used a pine branch to sweep out the hoofprints left by the Ovaro and the two Indian ponies. He worked his way toward Victoria, eliminating as much as possible every sign of their passing.

When he mounted the pony again, he led the way

carefully, picking a path that took them over stretches of rock and harder ground where they left few tracks. The disadvantage was that such care took time, which was in short supply.

After Fargo and Victoria had gone a mile or so from the valley where Fort Newcomb was located, he increased the pace and worried less about leaving sign. Speed was more important now.

Keeping the Rockies to their left, the two riders hustled northward through the foothills. More mountains rose off to the right. Fargo recognized them as the Castle Range and the Crazy Range. If he and Victoria kept going, they would reach the Missouri River in a day or two and could follow it all the way to Fort Benton. There was no danger of them getting lost; he had ridden through this country many times before.

Fargo didn't slow down until he heard Victoria let out a groan behind him. He pulled the pony to a walk and turned to look at her.

"Are you all right?"

"I . . . I've never ridden this much before," she said as she drew alongside him on the Ovaro. "It's rather painful."

Fargo thought about it for a moment, then said, "We'll take it easier for a while. We've put a good bit of distance between ourselves and the fort."

"You don't think the Indians will be able to find us now?"

Fargo knew there was a chance his maneuvers had thrown Broken Hand off their trail, but they couldn't count on that. "I don't know," he answered honestly. "But I know we have to rest these horses every now and then if we want them to keep going."

Victoria nodded gratefully and stretched in the saddle, trying to ease her sore muscles. She would really hurt by the next morning, Fargo thought.

After they had ridden for a while in silence, Victoria said, "I know who you are, you know. You're one of Tom's friends."

"That's right," Fargo said. If she felt like talking about what had happened, maybe that would be a good thing. "And you're his wife."

"Yes." Her voice caught a little as she added, "I *was* his wife."

Fargo didn't say anything.

After a moment, Victoria drew a deep breath and was able to go on. "I know Tom wrote to you and asked you to come up to the fort. I'm afraid I was the reason he wrote you that letter."

That surprised Fargo a little. He turned his head and looked at her.

"Tom was going to ask you to take me back east. I'm from St. Louis. That's where we met last year, before he was assigned to the new fort. Fort Newcomb." There was a bitter edge to her voice as she spoke the name.

"The two of you must've had what they call a whirlwind courtship," Fargo said.

Victoria nodded. "It was. We were married six weeks after we met. And we were very happy together, for a while."

"Then the Army sent him up here to Montana," Fargo guessed.

"That's right. Tom suggested that I stay in St. Louis, but I wouldn't hear of it. After all, we were newlyweds. I insisted that he bring me along."

The Army tried to discourage wives from accompanying their husbands to frontier postings, but there was no regulation against it. Sometimes it worked out, sometimes it didn't. From what Victoria Landon had said so far, in this case it hadn't worked out very well.

"I hated it," she continued bluntly. "The squalor, the isolation, the danger, all of it."

Fargo couldn't argue with her about the isolation and the danger, but he didn't see how anybody could apply the word "squalor" to their surroundings. Majestic snow-capped mountains, lush valleys, clear cold streams. . . . This country was in many ways heaven on earth as far as he was concerned. Every area of the frontier, from the Rio Grande to Canada, had both its beauties and its dangers, and Fargo would never feel at home anywhere else.

Victoria saw things differently, though, and that was her right.

Fargo said, "What were you going to do?"

"We weren't happy in our marriage anymore. We fought all the time. Tom thought it would be best if I went back home, and I did, too. I . . . don't know if we would have gotten a divorce. It's possible."

"And he wanted me to take you there."

"That's right. He wanted me safely away from the fort before winter set in."

It was almost too late for that—probably because it had taken a while for Tom Landon's letter to catch up to him, Fargo thought. And as it turned out, winter hadn't been the first danger to threaten Victoria.

"If it's not too difficult to talk about it, can you tell me what happened today?"

"It's difficult, all right," she said with a sigh, "but I can do it. Tom had gotten reports that a group of hostiles was in the area, and he was going to send out a patrol to look for them. But before he could, they attacked the fort. I'm not really sure how it started. All I know is that I heard shouts and gunshots, and when I ran out of our quarters, I saw Indians fighting with some of the troopers over by the blacksmith shop. I ran as fast as I could to Tom's office."

Fargo nodded. Broken Hand and his warriors couldn't have ridden up the valley toward the fort without being spotted by the sentries. Even greenhorns would have seen a mounted war party of that size.

But they could have approached the fort on foot, keeping under cover so well that even in broad daylight they couldn't be seen. They wouldn't have revealed themselves until they were close enough to start killing the cavalrymen. The troopers had been taken by surprise; Fargo was able to tell that by the way the corpses were scattered all over the fort. The only concentration of resistance had been at the headquarters building.

Victoria went on, "Once Tom saw what was going on, he took me into his office and told me he had a hiding place for me. You saw it yourself, under that trapdoor. He put me in there and told me to stay put, no matter what I heard going on outside. I . . . I promised him I would."

Fargo knew that Tom Landon had been trying to save his wife, but in a way he hadn't done her any kindness. If the soldiers were unable to repulse the attack, as had happened, then even if the raiders hadn't burned down the fort, Victoria would have been left on her own hundreds of miles away from anywhere approaching civilization. She would have either starved to death, died from exposure to the elements, been killed by wild animals, or fallen afoul of other Indians.

But Fargo supposed that she would have had a slim chance of survival, and that was what Tom Landon had been banking on. Any chance was better than none.

"I know you told him you'd stay put, but you must have smelled the smoke once the building caught on fire."

She nodded. "Yes, I . . . I panicked when I smelled the smoke. I tried to get out. But the door was stuck. I started yelling and pushing on it, and it finally came loose. I was trying to climb out when you came in and got me." She paused and then added, "Thank you. You saved my life. I know that."

"You're welcome. I'm just sorry I didn't get there sooner."

"Don't be. Then those savages would have killed you, too, and we'd both be dead. I'd rather be alive. Lord help me, I'm sorry about . . . about Tom and all those other men . . . but I'd rather be alive."

Fargo nodded slowly. It took some honesty to admit such a thing. He wasn't sure that he liked Victoria Landon, but he could respect the fact that she was glad to be alive.

Fargo judged that they had taken it easy long enough, so he increased the pace again. The Ovaro was almost tireless, though like any living creature he had his limits. The Indian ponies had also been bred to run long and hard. Fargo and Victoria pushed on as the day waned.

Not until it was almost dark did Fargo call another halt. He stopped where a rocky bluff bulged out from the side of a hill and formed a cavelike hollow at its base. "We'll spend the night here," he announced.

Victoria looked around; Fargo could tell she wasn't impressed by his choice, but they weren't likely to find a better place.

He had to help her down from the saddle. As his hands clasped her slender waist, he felt the play of muscles under her clothing. Her petticoats rustled as he put her on the ground.

Even though his hands didn't linger on her body, he was conscious of how close she stood to him. He shoved that thought out of his mind. She had been married to a friend of his, and had been a widow for only a matter of hours.

Still, even showing the strain of fear and exhaustion, Victoria was an attractive woman. There was no point in denying that, even though Fargo intended to treat her with the respect that the circumstances demanded, and that came naturally to him.

He got out his bedroll and spread it on the rocky ground at the base of the bluff. "Sit down and rest," he told her. "I'll tend to the horses."

She sank down gratefully, wincing as her sore bottom touched the ground. Fargo looked away so she wouldn't see him grin. He hobbled the two ponies so they wouldn't wander off, then unsaddled and rubbed down the Ovaro. He took the blankets and pads off the ponies and gave them the same treatment.

Enough grass remained to give the animals sufficient graze, and there was water close by in the form of a narrow stream that trickled out from a crack at the base of the bluff. Fargo refilled his canteen, got some jerky from his saddlebags, and went over to sit next to Victoria.

"Have a drink," he said as he handed the canteen to her. "And then you need to eat something."

"What is that?" she asked dubiously as she eyed the strip of jerky he held out to her. "It looks like a piece of leather."

"Tastes about like it, too," Fargo said with a grin. "Seriously, it's not that bad, but you have to have strong teeth to eat it. It's called jerky. Tear off a little strip with your teeth and chew on it a while. Sooner or later it'll soften up enough for you to eat it."

She looked doubtful, but after she had taken a long swallow of water from the canteen, she took the jerky and did as he told her. She made a face as she started to chew.

"Are you sure about this?" she asked thickly around the dried meat.

Fargo nodded. "Just keep at it," he said encouragingly. He bit off a piece for himself and settled down to chew it.

Without being too obvious about it, he studied her face in the fading light of dusk. Like the rest of her, it was slender, but the features were well formed. Her eyes, he had noticed earlier, were brown. Under the right circumstances, she would be beautiful, he sensed. As it was, she was damned attractive.

He could tell from the set of her mouth that she could probably be stubborn when she wanted to. She didn't strike him as weak, despite her complaints and the fact that she had fainted earlier.

"What are you looking at?" she demanded abruptly when she had finally swallowed the first bite of jerky.

"You," Fargo said, his voice blunt.

"Well, stop it. You're making me uncomfortable."

"I don't mean to. I was just thinking that you and Tom were probably a pretty good match."

"We were . . . at first."

"Shame it didn't last."

Her eyes narrowed. "Look, Mr. Fargo, I'm grateful for everything you've done. But that doesn't give you any right to pass judgment on me. You don't know all that went on between Tom and me. You didn't even know he was married, did you?"

"No," Fargo admitted, "I didn't."

"Tom Landon was a good man. I never denied that. If things had been different, I've no doubt I would have been happily married to him for the rest of my life."

"But you couldn't stand living out here."

"Don't say it like it's such a crime! Damn it, Fargo—"

There was that fire he thought he had seen in her. He held up a hand to forestall her angry protest.

"You're right," he told her. "It's none of my business. I owe it to Tom, though, to do my best to get you safely out of this mess. I think that's what he'd want."

She didn't respond for a moment, then said grudgingly, "I appreciate that." She bit into the jerky and with a savage twist of her head pulled off another strip of it.

They finished their meager supper in silence. The air continued to grow colder, and finally Victoria asked, "Are you going to build a fire?"

Fargo shook his head. "Too dangerous tonight. Broken Hand could be close enough behind us to see the light. If we can keep on giving him the slip, then it'll probably be safe to have a fire at night."

"But isn't the temperature liable to get down below freezing?"

"It sure might. These blankets will keep us warm, though, and I've got a sheepskin coat if you need to borrow it."

"We have to share the blankets?"

"I'll be a gentleman," Fargo promised with a chuckle. "And by morning, you'll be grateful for a little body heat. So will I."

"All right. But I'm going to hold you to that part about being a gentleman."

By the time they finished eating, night had fallen, and there was nothing to do except crawl into the bedroll and try to get some sleep. Fargo knew the Ovaro would alert him if anyone came sneaking around the camp. He rolled onto his side and pulled the blankets tight around him.

Victoria lay on her side, facing away from him. Her long, slender body was pressed against him. She was stiff, and Fargo knew the situation was awkward. Gradually, though, she relaxed, and after a while he heard her breathing grow deep and regular. She was asleep, claimed by the exhaustion that the day had forced on her.

Fargo dozed off, too, and gradually slipped into a deep, dreamless sleep. He didn't awaken until he became aware that Victoria had rolled over and pressed her face against his broad chest. She was crying, and she shook and shuddered as she sobbed. Fargo put his arms around her and held her.

"Tom . . . Tom . . ." she said. "Oh, my God, I'm so sorry. . . ."

Fargo was glad that she was grieving at last. She had kept herself tightly under control during the day as they were fleeing from Broken Hand's war party. She'd had to. There had been no time for her to give in to her sorrow.

But now it was good for her to get it all out. Fargo put a hand on her head and murmured, "It's all right." That made her cry even harder.

Finally the sobs died away to sniffles, and she fell asleep again. Fargo kept his arms around her, and after a while he slept again, too. This time, it was morning before he awoke.

The sun hadn't quite peeked over the mountains to the east, but it was close enough so that the sky was rosy with its approach. Fargo saw that Victoria had gotten up. He lay in the blankets and watched her walk stiffly over to the stream. She moaned softly as she knelt down to get a drink and then splashed cold water on her face. She reached behind her and loosened the braid. She ran her fingers through her long brown hair and shook her head until the strands hung freely about her shoulders. When she turned back toward him, Fargo saw that she was even prettier with her hair down that way.

"You're awake," she said.

"And you're in pain," Fargo said as she sat up. His breath fogged in front of his face.

"Horses are the devil in disguise." She rubbed her tender backside.

"We'd be in a bad fix without them."

"True. Did you . . . sleep well last night?"

"Just fine," Fargo said.

"Nothing disturbed you?"

He knew what she was talking about. Perhaps she wondered if she had dreamed the whole thing.

"Nothing bothered me," he told her honestly.

"I had . . . bad dreams."

"I'm not surprised. It was a hell of a thing you went through yesterday." Fargo pushed the blankets aside and stood up. "A lot of women wouldn't have been strong enough to make it."

"I'm strong enough," Victoria said, a hint of stubborn defiance in her voice. "I'll be all right."

"Never figured otherwise," Fargo said.

Breakfast was more creek water and jerky. "I thought you said there was plenty of game around here," Victoria commented as she gnawed the leatherlike meat.

"We don't want to be doing any shooting that we don't have to," Fargo explained. "Sound travels a long way out here. Maybe when we stop tonight I'll rig a snare, and by tomorrow morning we'll have a rabbit we can cook."

"You'll build a fire tomorrow?"

"We'll see," Fargo said.

After they had eaten, he got the horses ready to travel. Victoria was reluctant to climb back into the saddle but she did it, after some complaining.

Fargo had already scanned the countryside as best he could. He saw no sign of pursuit. In fact, the only movements he spotted were a small herd of elk about a mile away in some trees, and beyond them a bear poking around on a hillside. It wouldn't be very many days before that bear retreated to his den to hibernate for the winter.

An eagle wheeled through the sky high overhead as Fargo and Victoria moved out. "Where exactly are we going?" she asked.

"Fort Benton, up on the Missouri River. It's not a military post. It belongs to the American Fur Company. But it's the biggest settlement in this part of the territory."

"That's a long way away, isn't it?"

"Between a hundred and fifty and two hundred miles from here," Fargo agreed.

"How long will it take to get there?"

"A couple of weeks—maybe a week and a half if we don't run into any trouble."

Fargo didn't mention it, but he didn't expect the weather to hold for two more weeks. Even if they had lost Broken Hand, in all likelihood they would run into a storm on the way to the fort. If that happened, they would have to find a place to hole up and wait it out.

Victoria really needed a coat. She could wrap a blanket around herself and make do that way, but it would be better if she had a real coat.

Fargo suddenly remembered something he had heard at Fort Laramie. Someone had mentioned that a trading post had been established up here the previous summer. He didn't know exactly where it was, and the trader might have closed up and gone back to St. Louis or wherever he came from for the winter, but at least it was a possibility. If the trading post was still in business, he could get a coat or a buffalo robe for Victoria there, and maybe stock up on the supplies they would need, too.

He didn't say anything about it to her. He didn't want to get her hopes up, because it was entirely possible nothing would come of the idea. But still, Fargo felt a little better as they rode north.

Nothing was said about the way Victoria had cried

in the night or how Fargo had comforted her. Fargo was perfectly willing to leave his thoughts on the matter unspoken. It seemed to him, though, that Victoria was a bit more comfortable around him today. She even smiled at him a time or two.

But most of the time she wore a pained expression. Fargo could have told her that her sore muscles were going to get even worse before they got better, but what was the point of that?

He kept an eye on their back-trail as they rode, but as the day passed, there was still no sign of Broken Hand and the other Crow warriors. It was hard to believe they had given the Indians the slip, but Fargo allowed himself to hope that was the case. Anyway, it was time the warriors headed for their lodges for the winter, instead of gallivanting around the mountains looking for somebody to kill.

During the day, Fargo called several halts so they could rest. He was fairly pleased with the progress they were making—enough so that when Victoria let out an involuntary groan late that afternoon, Fargo was willing to stop for the day. He started looking for a suitable place to make camp.

He found a hollow on top of a hill that was surrounded by trees. When he had tended to the horses, he picked up some rocks and banked them in a circle, then built a small fire inside the circle. It gave off only a tiny amount of smoke, and the rocks hid the flames. Victoria huddled over it, pulling a blanket tight around her as she tried to get what warmth she could from the fire.

"Thank you," she said to Fargo. "I feel a little better already."

"I'll see about making that snare," he told her. "Some fresh meat in the morning will make you feel even better."

He used his Arkansas toothpick to cut some slender

branches from the trees and rig the snare. He had already spotted some rabbit tracks and was hopeful that come morning they would have a nice fat hare to roast.

Fargo was walking back toward Victoria when he saw an Indian step out of the trees behind her.

3

Fargo stopped in his tracks, his hand going to the butt of the Colt on his hip. The Henry rifle was propped against the Ovaro's saddle where it lay on the ground only a few feet from Victoria, but she had no idea the Indian was behind her.

Fargo was ready to draw and fire, but he stopped with his hand on the revolver as he saw that the Indian was an old man and wore no war paint. He shuffled forward, and finally Victoria heard the sound of his buckskin moccasins on the ground. She turned to look over her shoulder, saw the Indian, and screamed. She lunged toward the Henry.

"No!" Fargo said as he quickly stepped forward. "Wait, Victoria!"

As far as he could see, the old man was unarmed and didn't even have a bow and arrow. He was short and stocky, with a round face and a braid of hair hanging on either shoulder. Each was thickly shot through with gray.

Fargo could tell from the beadwork on the man's buckskins that he was Shoshone. The Shoshone were a peaceful people most of the time, though they would fight, and fight fiercely, if they were forced into it.

The old man stopped and held up a hand, palm

out, in the universal sign of peace. Fargo returned the gesture.

"My God, Skye, why don't you shoot him?" Victoria demanded anxiously.

"No need to," Fargo replied without taking his eyes off the Shoshone. "He's a friend."

"You mean you *know* him?"

"Nope, never saw him before in my life. But if he wanted trouble, he wouldn't have just walked up to us like this."

The Shoshone nodded. "This is right. Two Bears wants only peace."

Fargo came closer to him and said, "You speak the white man's tongue?"

"I learned it as a child from the Black Robes."

Fargo knew what the Shoshone was talking about. Missionaries, mostly French-Canadian Jesuits, had come to this part of the country back in the Shining Times, following in the footsteps of the fur trappers who had been the first white men to see this wild land. The missionaries had been basically unsuccessful at converting the so-called heathens, but they had managed to teach a lot of Indians to speak at least a little English.

Fargo saw that the Shoshone's features were drawn tight with strain, and the man's normally ruddy skin had a grayish cast to it. Something was wrong with him. Fargo looked closer and saw a dark stain on the left side of the Indian's buckskin shirt.

"You are hurt, Grandfather," he said.

Two Bears shrugged. "A scratch, that is all."

But even as he spoke, his eyes rolled up in his head and he toppled over backward, out cold.

Or dead. Fargo hoped that wasn't the case.

He sprang to the old Indian's side and knelt there to check for a pulse. Victoria scrambled to her feet and moved away, putting some distance between her and the Shoshone. "Is . . . is he . . . ?"

"He's alive," Fargo said. He pulled up the shirt to check on the old man's injury. "He's got a bullet hole through his side. The wound's not very deep, but he lost enough blood so that he finally passed out."

"What are we going to do with him?"

"Patch him up as best we can, I suppose."

Victoria crossed her arms over her chest and frowned. "Why do we have to help him?" she demanded. "He's an Indian. He's just like those savages who killed . . . who killed Tom and every other man at the fort."

Fargo shook his head. "Not hardly. Those were Crow. This old boy's a Shoshone. They're friendly to the whites, at least most of the time."

Two Bears was also outside the usual Shoshone hunting grounds, and Fargo wondered what he was doing over here on this side of the mountains. But he could get an answer to that question later, after he had tended to the bullet wound.

Using a wet cloth, he cleaned away the blood. From the looks of the holes in Two Bears' torso, the bullet had struck him from behind, burrowed a path an inch or two below the skin, and then burst out the front. Fargo packed both ends of the wound with moss, covered them with pads cut from one of the blankets, and then tightly tied the makeshift bandages in place.

Victoria stood by watching in disapproving silence. Fargo didn't care whether she liked the idea or not; he wasn't going to let a man bleed to death when there was something he could do about it.

When he was finished, he got the canteen and gave Two Bears a drink of water. A shot of whiskey might have been better, but Fargo didn't have any.

The Shoshone stirred and let out a groan. His eyes flickered open.

"You help . . . Two Bears?" he managed to say.

"That's right. You just rest now, Grandfather. You'll be fine." Fargo paused, then added, "Before you do, though, can you tell me who shot you?"

The old man gave a weary shake of his head. "I do not know. I did not see them. I heard a shot and then I was struck."

"When was this?"

"Earlier . . . today. Before the sun . . . stood at its highest in the sky."

That morning, then, Fargo thought. That agreed with his estimation, based on how the wound looked.

"Did you have a horse?"

Two Bears nodded. "I fell when I was shot. The horse . . . ran away. I do not know where it is."

That was enough questions. Fargo said, "All right, old-timer. Just take it easy for a while now." He lifted Two Bears' head and slipped a folded blanket under it. Two Bears closed his eyes, and a moment later Fargo could tell that he had slipped into a natural sleep.

"I hope you're not expecting me to share our blankets with *him,*" Victoria said. "I can smell him from here. He stinks."

"That's bear grease you smell," Fargo explained. "They use it on their hair and their bodies. You get used to the smell."

"I don't think I ever would."

She'd be surprised at what a person could get used to, Fargo thought. He said, "The horse blankets will keep him warm, and he won't mind."

"Will he . . . be all right?"

Fargo thought he heard some grudging concern in Victoria's voice. He said, "He should be, unless that wound festers. I would have liked to pour some whiskey through it, but we don't have any. The bleeding had already stopped, so really what he needs now is plenty of rest, along with some food when he wakes up."

"Who you think shot him?"

Fargo shook his head. "I don't know. Could have been a Crow or a Blackfoot out hunting. Those two bunches hate each other, but they don't like anybody else much, either. Or it could have been a white man—some trapper or trader who hasn't headed back east for the winter yet."

"Whoever it was, do you think he poses any threat to us?"

Her mind was quick, he had to give her credit for that. "No way of knowing. But since he's a back-shooter, I'd just as soon steer clear of him."

Night was falling rapidly now. Fargo and Victoria sat beside the tiny fire and chewed on jerky while Two Bears slept. Once it was dark, they huddled together in the bedroll again.

"You were a perfect gentleman last night, just as you promised," she said.

"I'm a man of my word," Fargo said dryly.

"I expect you to continue acting that way."

"Yes, ma'am."

She sniffed a little and turned her back to him. Fargo grinned as he pillowed his head on his hat and closed his eyes.

He slept soundly for several hours, and when he came awake, it was with the instant alertness common to the true frontiersman. He listened for any sounds of trouble, but the Ovaro stood quietly nearby, telling Fargo that no unwanted intruders were skulking around the campsite.

Then Victoria moaned and shifted under the blankets, pressing her backside against Fargo's groin and rubbing it back and forth.

In that first moment of waking, all his senses had been turned outward, seeking danger in the darkness.

Now he concentrated on what was closer at hand—literally. While he was sleeping, his arm had slipped around Victoria's slim form, and he found that his hand had come to rest on her right breast.

The mound of female flesh was firm and seemed to grow even more taut under his touch. Fargo knew he should take his hand away, but he let it stay where it was for a moment. He felt her nipple hardening against his palm.

Her hips began to rotate as she pressed back into him, molding her lower regions to his. Fargo's body responded. His manhood stiffened and throbbed.

She had to be able to feel his reaction against the soft, round curves of her backside, Fargo thought. Another quiet moan came from her throat. She reached up, caught hold of his hand, and pushed it harder against her breast.

Was she awake or asleep? Did she know what she was doing, or was she lost in some dream of making love to her late husband? Fargo couldn't answer those questions, and for one of the few times in his life, he wasn't sure what to do.

If she was asleep and he spoke to her, woke her up, she would realize what she was doing and be mortified. Either that, or she would be furious and accuse him of taking advantage of her. But if she was already awake, maybe she didn't want him to know that. Maybe she *wanted* him to think she was asleep.

Or maybe she just wanted him. . . .

Fargo grimaced. These circumstances were just too damned complicated. As much as he wanted to pull up her dress and plunge his shaft into her, he couldn't take the chance that she was really asleep. Taking her that way would be almost like rape. And if she was awake . . . well, he wasn't sure he wanted *that* complication, either. Not when they still had a long way to go before they would be safe.

He pulled his hand away from her breast, snorted as if he were half-waking from sleep, and rolled over, putting his back to her.

His ears were keen enough to hear the sigh that came from her lips, but he still couldn't tell if she was awake or not. Best not to think about it, he told himself. He closed his eyes.

But it was a while before he drifted off into slumber again.

Victoria didn't say anything the next morning about what had happened the night before. That was getting to be a habit, Fargo reflected. He was curious about what the next night would bring.

Two Bears was awake and as hungry as his namesake. Fargo thought that was a good sign. A man who was really sick usually didn't have such a good appetite.

The snare Fargo had set the evening before had a rabbit in it. He skinned the animal and soon had it roasting over the small fire.

The old Shoshone gnawed happily on a rabbit haunch when it was done. Fargo hunkered on his heels beside him and said, "The Shoshone hunting grounds are a good ways west of here, Grandfather. What are you doing in these parts, especially with winter coming on?"

"I left my people," Two Bears replied. A haughty note came into his voice as he went on, "My sons and their wives think I am an old man and good for nothing. They wished for me to leave, so that I would not be a burden on them when the snows come."

Fargo frowned. That didn't sound like typical Indian behavior. They generally honored their old people and tried to make life easy for them, at least to a point. When an Indian warrior sensed death approaching, he would sometimes leave the tribe so as to enter the spirit world alone, but Two Bears didn't seem to be anywhere near that point.

"So I took my pony and I rode away," Two Bears continued.

"You left without a gun or a bow?"

"I had a bow and a quiver of arrows. When I was shot . . . when I fell from my pony . . . I must have dropped them." Two Bears frowned and shook his head. "I . . . I do not remember. . . ."

"That's all right," Fargo told him. "We're headed for Fort Benton, and we've got an extra pony. You can come along with us."

Standing a few yards away, Victoria shifted her feet and cleared her throat. She frowned at Fargo. He ignored her as he leaned forward to check on Two Bears' wounds.

"Those bullet holes look pretty good, considering," he said. "Do you think you'll be up to riding today?"

"Two Bears can ride," the Shoshone declared.

That was good, Fargo thought, because he didn't like the idea of waiting around. While it was true they hadn't seen any signs of pursuit from Broken Hand and his band, that didn't mean the Crow war party wasn't behind them somewhere, searching for them.

"I've heard that there's a trading post somewhere up here in these parts. Do you know if that's true?"

Two Bears shook his head. "This land is new to Two Bears. Never have I ridden it before."

"Well, we'll keep looking," Fargo said. "Either way, we'll be moving in the right direction."

Two Bears looked from Fargo to Victoria and back again. "Why are you and your squaw here?"

"I am *not* his squaw," Victoria burst out.

Fargo tried not to grin. "As I said, we are on our way to Fort Benton." He grew more solemn as he went on, "The lady was at Fort Newcomb with her husband. Broken Hand's Crows attacked the fort and killed everyone except her."

Two Bears nodded. "I have heard of this Broken Hand. He is a fierce war chief and lives only to kill his enemies."

"That's about the size of it," Fargo agreed. "Come to think of it, you might be better off if you didn't travel with us. I killed a couple of Broken Hand's warriors, so he's liable to come after us. I can give you one of the ponies—"

Two Bears rejected the offer with a shake of his head. "You saved the life of Two Bears. I will go with you, my friend. . . ." He hesitated, clearly waiting for Fargo to introduce himself.

"Skye Fargo," the Trailsman supplied. "And the lady is Mrs. Landon."

Two Bears barely glanced at Victoria. "Thank you, Skye Fargo. My life is now yours."

Fargo didn't waste time arguing with the old man. He didn't know if he had really saved Two Bears' life or not—the Shoshone might have survived the wound without Fargo's assistance—but since Two Bears felt that way, it became a point of honor to him. A blood debt. He would do anything for Fargo now.

Fargo patted Two Bears on the shoulder and straightened. "I'll see to the horses," he said. With a look at Victoria, he added, "We'll be riding in a few minutes, if there's anything you need to do first."

She nodded, blushing slightly, and withdrew into some bushes. Fargo went over to the stallion and the two Indian ponies to get them ready to ride.

Victoria couldn't restrain a groan as she climbed into the saddle. As they started moving, however, Fargo thought she didn't seem quite as uncomfortable as she had been the day before. She was getting used to riding quicker than he had expected, which was a good thing because they still had plenty of it to do.

Two Bears had refused an offer of help when it came time to climb onto the pony he was riding. Fargo got the impression that the old Shoshone was very proud and didn't like to accept assistance from anyone. He wondered if that was the real reason Two Bears had left his people and wandered east across the Rockies. Maybe his family hadn't chased him away at all.

Around midmorning, they reached the Missouri River. Here in the higher country, the Missouri wasn't wide, flat, muddy, and slow-moving like it was farther downstream. It was narrower and flowed faster as it followed a course between rocky banks.

If the trading post Fargo had heard about was actually up here somewhere, likely it would be located on the river. Many such posts had been built in the forty or fifty years that fur trapping had been going on in the mountains. Some of the posts had been abandoned and had fallen into ruin; others had been attacked and burned down by Indians. And a very few, such as Fort Benton, had been able to survive and had grown into what passed for towns in this untamed Montana country.

Two Bears looked around as they rode and announced, "This is Blackfoot hunting ground. If Crow warriors follow us, they will have to fight Blackfoot as well."

"That won't stop 'em if they really want our scalps," Fargo said. "The Crow and the Blackfoot have been at war with each other as far back as I can remember. Broken Hand might be even more likely to chase us if he thought he could kill some Blackfeet in the bargain."

"This is true," Two Bears agreed solemnly.

They followed the west bank of the river for the rest of the day. Fargo was pleased with the progress they were making, but he continued checking the sky, watching for gathering storm clouds. He kept a close eye on their back-trail, too, unwilling to believe just yet that Broken Hand had given up.

When it came time to stop for the night, Fargo led them away from the Missouri and chose a place to camp in some trees where they wouldn't be so easy to see. Again, though it was obvious the old Shoshone was stiff and sore from his bullet wound, Two Bears stubbornly refused any help getting down from his pony. So did Victoria Landon. It would be an interesting contest, Fargo thought as he grinned to himself, to see just which one of them could be the most mule-headed.

He had saved some of the roasted rabbit from that morning, and they ate it for supper. Victoria hadn't been very happy about eating wild game, but tonight she seemed to be hungry enough not to care about such things. She ate as eagerly as Fargo and Two Bears.

Fargo put out the small fire when they were finished eating. Two Bears curled up in the horse blankets and went to sleep right away, snoring softly. Fargo and Victoria crawled into the bedroll. Fargo thought about standing guard, but the Ovaro was the best sentry around. He knew the stallion would let him know if anyone or anything approached.

"How many more days will it take us to get there?" Victoria asked sleepily as she lay facing away from him. Fargo knew she was talking about Fort Benton.

"Hard to say. Five or six, anyway. Maybe seven or eight."

"It seems so far away. We're so alone, so far from everything. . . . It seems almost like we're the last people alive on earth."

Fargo knew that feeling. The vast remoteness of the frontier produced it in everyone from time to time. But though this land was indeed sparsely populated, they were far from alone out here. Unfortunately, most of the area's inhabitants posed a threat to them.

Victoria dozed off. Fargo stayed awake for a time, listening to all the little sounds of the night, but finally he drifted into slumber as well.

For the third night in a row, he was awakened from sleep by Victoria. He was aware of it when she turned over so that she faced him under the blankets. He wasn't sure what she was going to do, but this time there was no doubt that she was awake. She whispered his name: "Skye . . ."

And then her mouth found his in a hot, urgent kiss. Fargo returned the kiss, sliding his arms around her to pull her closer to him as he did so.

Ever since he had met her, Victoria Landon had been rather cool toward him—had even seemed angry with him much of the time despite the fact that he had saved her life. Of course, there had been those moments the previous night when she had writhed against him and pressed his hand to her breast, but he still didn't know if she had been aware of what she was doing.

She was aware of what she was doing now; Fargo had no doubt about that. Her lips opened eagerly as his tongue stroked them. Their tongues met and fenced sensuously.

Fargo's hand slid down her back to the curve of her hips. She pressed her pelvis to him, grinding it against his thickening shaft. As he grew harder, Victoria reached between them, her hand darting down to grope his manhood through the buckskin trousers.

A part of Fargo's brain was still cautious. Victoria was a very recent widow, after all. If they both gave in to the passion they felt, would she regret it later?

Would she hate him or hate herself? Fargo didn't know, but it was clear that right here and now, Victoria wanted him to make love to her.

She broke the kiss and gasped, "Skye, I need you! Damn it, I need you inside me!"

Fargo trailed kisses over her cheeks and chin and the hollow of her throat. He moved his hand around, insinuated it between them, and cupped her left breast. His thumb found the hardening nubbin of her nipple and caressed it through the fabric of her dress.

Victoria's fingers worked at the buttons of his trousers. After a moment, she got them open and reached inside. Her hand closed around his shaft. Fargo's hips surged forward involuntarily at the warmth of her touch. She gasped again as she felt the length and heft of him.

Though it was difficult, Fargo paused to listen. He heard deep, regular breathing from Two Bears that told him the old Shoshone was still asleep. He heard a faint crunching that he knew came from the horses as they grazed unworriedly on the sparse grass under the trees. The night was calm, cold, and peaceful.

Fargo gave himself over to the arousal that grew within him as Victoria stroked his thick member. He reached down to pull up her skirt. Getting each other sufficiently undressed within the confines of the bedroll was a tricky business, but over the next few minutes, they managed. When Fargo finally laid bare Victoria's femininity, he rested the ball of his hand on her fur-covered mound and dipped his middle finger into her hot, slick core.

Her hips bucked upward as her heated juices coated his finger. He added a second finger and slid them back and forth inside her. She twisted her head from side to side in sheer pleasure. She wrapped both hands around his shaft and squeezed, milking him.

Fargo moved over her as she spread her legs in

wanton invitation. She sighed as his fingers slipped out of her, but the disappointment lasted only a second. Then he brought the head of his manhood to her opening and rubbed it up and down the already drenched folds of female flesh. Her hips came up as Fargo's drove down, and just like that his organ was fully sheathed inside her.

Some instinct warned him that she was about to cry out, so he kissed her to muffle the sound. She twined her arms around his neck and held him with incredible strength as her tongue speared into his mouth. She raised her knees and locked her ankles together behind his back as he pumped into her.

Fargo started off moving fairly slowly, but the pace of the age-old rhythm increased inexorably. Passion and desire burgeoned within each of them. Victoria's hips bucked off the ground as she met Fargo thrust for thrust.

The need for release grew stronger as their excitement built. Finally, Fargo felt his climax boiling up. He didn't even attempt to hold back, because he felt Victoria spasming underneath him as her own culmination rippled through her. With a final thrust, he buried his shaft inside her as deep as it would go and emptied himself into her.

When it was over, he rested his weight on his elbows and kissed her lightly. He felt her heart hammering where her breasts were flattened against his chest. Neither of them could speak for several moments.

When Victoria got her voice back, she said quietly, breathlessly, "Oh, Skye . . . you can't know . . . how much that meant to me. . . . I was afraid I would never . . . never know such a feeling again."

So that was it, Fargo thought. She was still afraid she was going to die out here, and she wanted to experience passion again while she still had the chance. It was a common enough reaction for people who found themselves in dangerous situations, and that need to reach out and grasp some of the essence of life overpowered everything else.

"I'm glad I was here," Fargo murmured as he nuzzled her jaw just under her ear.

"You don't think I'm a terrible person? That I was disloyal to . . . to Tom?"

Fargo raised himself up again so that he was looking down into her eyes in the starlight. "Tom Landon was a man who was full of human appetites himself," he said. "If he loved you, the last thing he would have wanted was to see you unhappy and scared."

She began to cry softly. "Thank you, Skye . . . for everything."

Fargo held her close, and after a while she went to sleep again. He was glad that he had been able to give her those moments when she could put all the fear and pain behind her.

But they were still a long way from being out of the woods. A lot could happen between here and Fort Benton.

4

Fargo was fairly sure Two Bears hadn't heard anything that had gone on between him and Victoria Landon the night before. The Shoshone certainly didn't say anything about it the next morning.

The bullet wounds in the old man's side were healing, Fargo saw when he checked them. He still wondered who had shot Two Bears, and why. He knew he might never find out the answer to those questions. If he didn't, he wouldn't lose any sleep over the matter . . . but he would still wonder about it.

He had rigged a snare the night before but hadn't caught anything in it, so they had a skimpy breakfast of jerky and then started riding north again, following the river.

Fargo estimated that in another couple of days they would reach the spectacular gorge known as the Gates of the Rocky Mountains. From there the river plunged down a long series of waterfalls until it reached the plains and curved northeast toward Fort Benton. The terrain around the falls was rugged and would take some time to cross.

Once they were past the falls, however, the going would be fairly easy. Though Fargo's attention was fixed firmly on their surroundings, a part of his brain ranged out far ahead of them, planning their route.

His ability to do that was one of the things that had led to him being known as the Trailsman.

Around midday, Fargo reined the pony he was riding to an abrupt halt as he spotted something up ahead. He motioned for Victoria and Two Bears to stop as well, and pointed at a thin tendril of smoke climbing into the sky.

"Is that from someone's campfire?" Victoria asked.

"More likely from that trading post I heard about," Fargo replied. "We'll take it easy when we get closer, just to make sure what we're getting into."

He had Victoria pull the Henry from its saddle sheath on the Ovaro and hand it to him. Holding the rifle ready across his body, Fargo rode on. To his right, the banks of the Missouri had narrowed and deepened, and the river roared as it flowed swiftly over its rocky streambed, twisting and turning through the rugged, pine-covered landscape.

Fargo rode around a bend in the river and saw a building on the west bank, about five hundred yards away. It was a good-sized log structure, with a stone chimney on either end. The smoke they had seen rose from one of the chimneys.

Logs had been split and cut into short lengths to form a series of steps that led down to the river, where a crude dock had been built. A couple of canoes were tied there, bobbing on the water. Beyond the big cabin were a couple of other buildings. Fargo pegged one of them as a smokehouse. He thought the other one was probably a drying shed where pelts could be cured.

He had seen trading posts like this before, little outposts of civilization in the midst of the wilderness. He relaxed a bit at the sight of this one. It was his hope that he and his companions could rest here for a short time and replenish their supplies before continuing on to Fort Benton. Two Bears might even decide to stay and spend the winter, if the owner of the post had no objection. There was no reason the Shoshone had to go on with Fargo and Victoria.

"My God, Skye, I wondered if we would ever make it. Do you think there might be a real bed in there?" she asked.

Fargo chuckled. "Something better than the ground, anyway. Come on."

As they rode closer he saw a small corral behind the main building. A couple of mules stood under a lean-to shed. As late in the season as it was, there wouldn't be any more fur business for the trader this year. They were lucky he hadn't pulled out yet. Of course, the trader might be the sort who sat out the winter up here. Some men liked the isolation.

A large dog came around the cabin and ran toward them, barking loudly. Something was strange about the animal, and Fargo had to look twice before he realized that it had only three legs. One of the rear ones was gone. But the dog seemed spry enough despite its handicap.

Attracted by the commotion of the barking, a man wearing buckskins and a shapeless felt hat stepped out of the cabin holding a shotgun. He was on the small side, with a shock of graying sandy hair and a bushy beard of the same color. He called, "Thor! Thor, come back here, you danged mutt!"

Fargo kept the rifle in plain sight but didn't make any threatening moves with it, as he led the small party up to the trading post. A board hung over the door, and words had been carved into it with a hot iron: *Poudre River Pete's*.

The dog ran to the man and stood beside him, growling at the strangers. The man regarded them intently but there was nothing hostile in his manner. He was just being careful, because that was the way to stay alive out here.

"Howdy," he said as they reined in. "Welcome to Poudre River Pete's."

Fargo nodded. "That would be you?"

"It would," the man replied. "Call me Pete. I come up here from Colorado to open a tradin' post."

"My name is Skye Fargo," the Trailsman introduced himself. "This is Mrs. Landon, and that's Two Bears."

Pete studied the old Indian. "Shoshone, ain't he?"

"I am Shoshone," Two Bears said with stiff dignity.

"Well, light and set, all of you," Pete invited. "You can put that big fella and them ponies in the corral around back. I'll fetch some grain for 'em." The dog growled again and Pete looked down. "Thor, hush up, dang it! These folks are friendly." He glanced at Fargo. "You *are* friendly, ain't you?"

"We're not looking for any trouble at all," Fargo assured the trader.

"That's good. Thor here, he's been a mite crotchety ever since a silvertip grizzly chewed his leg off. I reckon that'd make me a little touchy, too."

Fargo dismounted to lead the horses to the corral. Pete went with him after telling Victoria and Two Bears to go into the cabin and make themselves at home.

"Didn't really expect to see any more folks around here until next spring," Pete commented as he got a bag of grain from the shed and poured some of the feed into a trough for the horses.

"You're spending the winter here?" Fargo asked.

"Yep. My partner went to St. Looey with a load of plows to sell. He'll be back in the spring with fresh supplies. We figured one of us better stay to look after the place. Injuns might burn it down if they found it empty."

"You had any trouble with the Blackfeet or the Crows?"

Pete shook his head. "Nope, they've left me plumb

alone. Been lucky, I guess." He scratched at his beard. "Mind if I ask what you folks are doin' out here?"

"We're headed for Fort Benton. Mrs. Landon's had some trouble and needs a place to spend the winter." Fargo sketched in what had happened over the past few days.

Pete let out a low whistle when he heard about the massacre. "I knew there was a fort a ways south of here. From what I've heard of Broken Hand, I ain't surprised he wiped it out. He's supposed to be a mean son of a bitch."

"I'd just as soon not find out," Fargo said.

"You and me both, friend." Pete's eyes narrowed. "You say you reckon he might be trailin' you?"

"It's possible," Fargo said. "We haven't done you any favors by stopping here."

"Hell, I ain't worried about Broken Hand. If he shows up, Thor'll run him off like the varmint he is." Pete reached down to rub the big dog's head as Thor sat at his feet. "Won't you, boy?"

Thor licked Pete's hand.

With the horses taken care of, Fargo and the trader went back around the building to the door. It was closed against the wind, which was cold despite the sunshine. They went inside, stepping into cheery warmth.

A good-sized fire burned in the fireplace to the right, Fargo saw, and the heat it gave off more than made up for the occasional drafts that whistled through chinks in the log walls. Several thick rugs were laid out on the puncheon floor. Some of them had been woven by Indians, while others were made from bear hides. The chairs and the big table that sat in the middle of the room were crude and rough-hewn but perfectly functional. To the left were shelves where supplies and trade goods were kept, and in the back of the room was a long counter where Pete could lay out and inspect the beaver pelts he traded for in his business.

Victoria and Two Bears stood near the fireplace, warming themselves. Victoria smiled at Fargo and said, "I didn't realize just how cold I've been the past few days until I started to warm up."

Fargo thought she hadn't been cold at all in their bedroll the night before, but he didn't say anything about that. He joined them by the fire and held his hands out toward the flames. The heat felt good.

"Could I interest you folks in a drink?" Pete asked from behind them. "Well, not the Injun, of course, since redskins don't handle firewater very good."

The old Shoshone looked around. "Two Bears drink whiskey," he declared. "Two Bears drink whiskey just fine."

"No, sir," Pete said, gesturing with the bottle he had taken from under the counter in the back of the room. "I been accused of a heap o' bad things in my life, but one thing nobody'll ever accuse me of is sellin' whiskey to the Injuns!"

"What I'd really like if you've got it," Fargo said to change the subject, "is some hot coffee."

Pete grinned. "I got that, all right. Lemme put away this who-hit-John, and I'll get a pot to boilin'."

Fargo saw Two Bears watching as Pete replaced the whiskey bottle under the counter, and he told himself that he might want to keep an eye on the Shoshone, just to make sure that the old-timer didn't get into the liquor.

Soon the smell of brewing coffee filled the room, and Pete made things even more aromatic by heating up a pot of stew. When Fargo finished eating, he felt better than he had since before he'd heard those distant gunshots and seen the smoke spiraling up from Fort Newcomb as the outpost burned.

"How long you folks plan to stay?" Pete asked as

they sat at the long table, sipping the last of their coffee from tin cups.

"Mrs. Landon and I will probably move on tomorrow," Fargo replied. He thought he saw a flash of disappointment in Victoria's eyes. She probably would have liked to stay here longer and rest after the arduous days on the trail, but they couldn't afford to do that—not as long as it was possible that Broken Hand was coming after them.

Pete gestured toward Two Bears with his cup. "What about the Injun?"

"Two Bears go with Fargo," the Shoshone answered before Fargo had a chance to reply.

"You don't have to, Two Bears," Fargo said. "You can spend the winter here at the trading post if you want. That is, if it's all right with Pete."

"Sure," the trader declared without hesitation. "Reckon I could do with the company. It'll be a long time until spring. Ol' Thor's a mighty good companion, but ever' now and again a fella gets to where he wants to hear a human voice."

"Two Bears go with Fargo," the old man repeated stubbornly. "Fargo save Two Bears' life."

"It's up to you," Fargo said. "I just wanted you to know that you've got a choice."

Two Bears nodded solemnly and crossed his arms over his chest, a signal that the discussion was over.

Thor's ears suddenly pricked up and the dog, which had been sitting by his master's chair, came up on all three of his legs. The fur on his back bristled as he looked toward the door. A low growl came from his throat.

"Thor? What in tarnation's got into you?" Pete asked. "You hear something?"

Fargo had heard it, too, even though he wasn't growling like the dog. "Riders coming," he said.

"Dang! This is my day for company, I reckon."

Pete got up and started toward the door. Fargo said sharply, "Wait a minute."

Pete stopped and looked at him with a frown, then understanding dawned on the trader's bearded face. "You think that might be Broken Hand?"

Fargo was on his feet. "It wouldn't be like a Crow war party to just ride up in the open like this." He snatched up the Henry rifle, which was lying on the table. "But it doesn't hurt to be careful."

"Damn right," Pete muttered as he got his shotgun from the counter in the back of the room.

The Shoshone stood up as well. "Give Two Bears a gun. Two Bears will fight for his friends."

Pete reached under the counter and brought up an old cap-and-ball pistol. "Here you go, Chief," he said as he walked over and handed the gun to Two Bears. "Be careful. It's loaded."

Two Bears grunted. "Gun no damn good if it's not loaded."

Victoria looked anxiously at Fargo. "Skye, do you really think it's the war party?"

"We'll find out in a minute," he told her. By now he could hear the hoofbeats of at least half a dozen horses. Broken Hand's war party had been much bigger than that, but these newcomers could be scouts from the main party.

Fargo motioned for Pete to go to the door, and moved over to one of the shuttered windows, ready to fling it open and blaze away with the Henry if he needed to. Thor began to bark as Pete reached for the latch. The trader looked down at the dog and said quietly, "Hush."

Then he turned the latch and threw the door open as the riders drew up outside.

Fargo was watching Pete's face. He saw the relief flood over the trader's features. Pete lifted a hand in greeting and called out cheerily, "Howdy, boys!" He stepped outside.

Fargo left the window and went to the door. When he looked out, he saw eight white men dismounting from lathered horses. They were all roughly dressed and heavily armed. Most had beards. One of them stepped forward and said to Pete, "Mighty glad we spotted the smoke from your chimney, friend. We didn't know there were any white men this side of Fort Benton."

"Yep. Poudre River Pete's my name, and this here is my tradin' post. Come on in. Stew's still hot, and I can brew up another pot of coffee."

The spokesman started toward the door, but he stopped short when he saw Fargo standing there, one shoulder propped against the jamb, the Henry held in his right hand with the barrel down along his leg.

The man was tall and powerful, with rusty red hair under a black hat and a tangled red beard. His face was craggy, the nose having been broken at least once. Eyes of a paler blue than Fargo's studied the Trailsman for a moment before the man gave a curt nod. "Howdy."

Fargo returned the nod and stepped back to let the red-bearded man lead his companions into the trading post.

Fargo had learned to listen to his instincts, and they told him that these men were not to be trusted. It wasn't just a matter of their appearance. Plenty of men on the frontier looked rough as cobs but were actually good-hearted and as honest as the day was long. What Fargo didn't like was the look in Redbeard's eyes. It was cold and hard and dangerous.

Redbeard hadn't missed the fact that Pete and Fargo were armed. He noticed the gun in Two Bears' hand, too. He went to the fireplace, took off his hat, ran his fingers through his longish hair and then turned to face the center of the room.

"Looks like you folks were expecting trouble."

"Nope," Pete answered quickly. "Just bein' careful."

Redbeard nodded. "Always a good thing to be." He put his hat back on. "Name's Smoky Jack Mallory." He waved a hand at the other men crowding into the room. "These are pards of mine . . . Burke, Gramlich, Trout, Tompkins, Shoemaker, Holmes, and McCollum."

Each man nodded in turn as Mallory introduced them. Some of them smiled, but the expressions weren't very friendly. More than one of them had naked lust in his eyes as he looked at Victoria Landon.

"You boys on your way to Idaho to look for gold?" Pete asked.

"That's right," Mallory responded, a little too quickly in Fargo's judgment. "We came to look for gold."

More than likely their intention was to rob the parties of wealth seekers on their way to Idaho. Fargo had run up against outlaw gangs many times in the past, and unless he missed his guess, Mallory and the other men fit that description just fine.

But they had seen that Fargo, Pete, and Two Bears were armed, so maybe they would decide against trying anything while they were here at the trading post. While it was true they outnumbered the others by more than two to one, men who rode the owlhoot trail usually liked to have the odds even more overwhelming in their favor.

"You said something about some coffee and stew?" Mallory went on.

"Sure thing," Pete said. "Just hold on a minute."

Fargo took Victoria's arm and led her back to the

counter in the rear of the room as the newcomers gathered around the table. Two Bears joined them, tucking the pistol behind his belt as he did so.

While Pete dished up stew for the strangers, Victoria said in a low voice to Fargo, "I didn't like the way those men were looking at me, Skye."

Fargo grunted. "I don't like much of anything about them. But we'll keep an eye on them, and they probably won't try anything."

"Two Bears not trust them," the old Shoshone rumbled.

Fargo nodded in agreement. "Like I said, we'll watch them."

Mallory and his men talked and laughed quietly among themselves as they ate. They seemed to be paying no attention to Fargo and the others now, but Fargo knew that wouldn't last. He caught Pete's eye, and when the trader came over, he asked, "Do you have a room where Mrs. Landon can get some rest?"

"Sure. You can have my room, ma'am. It ain't fancy, but it's got a bunk in it. Beats curlin' up on the floor in a bearskin robe."

"I wouldn't want to put you out of your room—" Victoria began.

"Oh, don't think nothin' of it." Pete grinned. "Heck, once you folks are gone, it'll make the winter pass a mite easier just knowin' such a pretty gal stayed here."

He took Victoria to a door at the far end of the room, away from the fireplace. There was another fireplace down at that end of the building, Fargo recalled, but no smoke had been coming from its chimney. Pete would have to kindle a fire in it to warm up the room for Victoria, but there was plenty of time for that before nightfall.

In fact, Fargo hoped that Mallory's bunch would

move on after they ate, since it was only early afternoon and they could put some more miles under their belt before camping for the night.

Mallory dashed that hope pretty quickly. When Pete came back from showing Victoria to the bedroom, Mallory said to him, "Reckon we'll bed down here tonight, mister." He didn't ask if that was all right.

"You'll have to sleep out here," Pete told him. "Ain't got no private rooms 'cept one, and the lady's usin' it."

"That's fine," Mallory said. "It'll beat sleeping on the trail."

Several of the men chuckled. Fargo didn't like the sound of it.

He was convinced that sooner or later, the outlaws would try to kill him, Pete, and Two Bears. Then they would take turns violating Victoria. They might take her with them when they left the trading post, or they might go ahead and kill her then, if they were tired of her. Either way, she would wind up dead, too.

Fargo meant to see to it that such things didn't happen. At the first sign of trouble, he planned to put a bullet through Smoky Jack Mallory's head. The rest of the gang might back off if their leader was dead.

When the men finished eating, some of them sat in front of the fire and rolled quirlies. Mallory was one of them. A couple leaned their chairs back against the wall and seemed to go to sleep. Three more got out a greasy deck of cards.

"We need somebody else to sit in on the game," one of them said. He looked at Fargo. "How about you, mister?"

A good game of poker was one of the things Fargo liked best in the world, but under these circumstances, he shook his head and said, "No thanks."

The three men frowned at him. Another of them said, "You reckon you're too good to play with us?"

"I never said that. I'm just not in the mood for cards right now."

The man looked at Two Bears. "How about you, Chief?"

Fargo wanted the Shoshone to turn them down, too, but before he could catch Two Bears' eye, the old-timer said, "Two Bears not a chief. Like to play poker, though. Five-card stud?"

One of the outlaws at the table grinned. "That's right. How'd you learn to play poker and talk English so good?"

"Black Robes teach Two Bears the white man's tongue. Learn to play poker from fur trappers." Two Bears took a seat at the table.

Fargo picked up one of the chairs, turned it around, set it near the table, and straddled it. He couldn't stop Two Bears from playing, but at least he could stay close by in case of trouble.

As the cards were being shuffled, one of the men asked, "Hey, Chief, what are you goin' to use for money? You got any wampum?"

Two Bears reached into a pocket. "Got white man's money." He slapped a twenty-dollar gold piece onto the table.

Fargo wondered where Two Bears had gotten the money but there was no chance to ask him. The outlaws laughed, and the one holding the deck began to deal.

Two Bears probably wouldn't be in the game very long, Fargo thought. He would probably lose that twenty dollars fairly quickly.

But to Fargo's surprise—and the surprise of the other men in the game—Two Bears played carefully and well, winning the first couple of hands to build up a small stake. Fargo watched closely and, as far as he could tell, the other men weren't cheating. Likely they had thought they wouldn't have to in order to take the old man's money.

The game continued as the afternoon passed. Two Bears lost some of the hands, but he won more of them. The pile of coins and wadded-up greenbacks in front of him grew steadily. Mallory and the other men came over to watch. So did Pete. Whatever murderous plans the outlaws might have had seemed to be forgotten, as everyone was engrossed in the game.

Fargo didn't let down his guard, though. His right hand was never far from the butt of his Colt.

"Damn it!" one of the outlaws burst out as he threw down his cards in disgust and Two Bears raked in another pot. "This redskin can't lose!"

"He's a lucky old son of a bitch. Ain't you, Chief?" another man gibed at the Shoshone.

"Lucky old son of bitch," Two Bears agreed solemnly.

One of the bystanders laughed and said, "You're a whole heap luckier than the last Injun we saw. Smoky Jack plugged him. Prettiest shot you ever did see. Must've been five hundred yards across a canyon, but Jack drew a bead on him and dropped him with one shot."

Fargo's jaw tightened. He saw Two Bears' eyes narrow and knew the Shoshone was thinking the same thing he was.

"When was this?" Fargo asked, making the question sound idly curious.

"A couple of days ago."

Fargo looked at Mallory. "You shot an Indian?"

Mallory shrugged. "Why not? What's one stinkin' redskin more or less? Besides, I needed to sight my rifle."

Anger welled up inside Fargo. He drew a tight rein on it. Mallory had no idea that the man he'd shot just for the pleasure of it was Two Bears. If Fargo had had any doubt about the sort of skunks that Mallory and his men were, this conversation had settled it.

Two Bears was as calm as ever, giving no sign of what he had learned about the attempt on his life. He continued to play.

The fact that his opponents in the game still hadn't resorted to cheating told Fargo that they planned on getting the money back. That was one more indication the outlaws intended to murder everyone else at the trading post. But they still didn't like being beaten, especially by an Indian. The atmosphere in the room was fast becoming tense and angry.

Mallory broke the tension a little by saying, "It'll be dark soon. Burke, you and Trout go see to the horses."

"Aw, they're probably all right, Jack," one of the men protested.

"Do like I told you, damn it," Mallory snapped. Clearly, the men didn't want to cross him, because they got up right away and went out of the cabin. Everyone else continued to watch the poker game.

Then one of the men who had gone outside let out a scream of agony. As everyone looked up, startled, the door burst open and one of the outlaws reeled into the cabin, blood welling from his mouth, the feathered shaft of an arrow protruding from his chest.

5

Everyone leaped up. Curses and shocked exclamations filled the air as the wounded man stumbled toward the table. He lost his balance and wheeled halfway around so that the others could see two more arrows sticking out of his back. More blood gushed from his mouth as he croaked, "Injuns!"

Then he pitched to the floor, dead.

The warning was unnecessary. Everyone in the trading post knew what had happened, even Victoria, who had heard the commotion and come out of the bedroom. When she saw the arrow-riddled corpse lying on the floor in a rapidly spreading pool of blood, she clapped her hands to her mouth and screamed.

Fargo didn't have time to comfort her now. He sprang to the open door and threw it shut. As he did so, an arrow whipped through the narrowing gap to hit the floor. Another arrow thudded into the closing door.

Fargo dropped the bar that kept the door from being opened. Instinctively taking command, he called out, "Get to the windows!"

The outlaws obeyed—even Smoky Jack Mallory, although he cast a slightly resentful glance toward the Trailsman. Fargo saw the look and knew Mallory didn't like the way he had taken charge.

He could worry about that later, Fargo thought—assuming any of them survived the attack on the trading post.

Those were Crow arrows sticking out of the dead man. Fargo knew that from the markings on them. He knew as well that Broken Hand's war party had finally caught up to them. The Crow war chief had to be happy. Not only had he found the man who had killed two of his warriors, but now he had the opportunity to murder several more of the hated white-eyes as well.

Fargo's Henry had a round in the chamber. He opened a shutter slightly and carefully peered out. None of the Indians were in sight, but he knew they were out there.

Suddenly a blood-curdling yell went up and several figures in feathers and buckskins charged from the brush along the river bank. Fargo brought the rifle to his shoulder and fired. More shots blasted from the other windows as Mallory's men opened up on the attacking Crows.

The war party had rifles, too. Shots rang out. Fargo heard slugs smashing into the thick log walls. The walls were sturdy enough to stop the bullets, but the shutters weren't. A couple of shots punched in to whine through the cabin.

Fargo glanced over his shoulder and saw Pete hustling Victoria behind the long counter. "Get down there on the floor, ma'am," he told her. "You ought to be safe there."

Safe from everything except the luckiest of bullets, Fargo thought. He turned his attention back to the outside as he worked the Henry's lever. Dusk was settling over the Montana landscape, which meant that the Indians were little more than shadowy shapes as they darted from tree to bush to tree, working their way closer to the trading post.

Fargo drew a bead, fired, and was rewarded by the

sight of a Crow warrior cartwheeling off his feet. The Indian came to a stop and lay still, either dead or badly wounded.

Fargo had brought in his saddlebags when he and his companions stopped at the trading post, so he had plenty of ammunition for his weapons. Mallory and his men hadn't done that. Their gear was still outside with their horses—which meant that by now it was in the hands of the war party.

He didn't know how well Pete was fixed for food and water, either. They might not be able to withstand a long siege.

Of course, a siege might not be what Broken Hand had in mind. The war party was large enough so that Broken Hand might not mind spending the lives of some of his men in order to overrun the trading post and slaughter everyone inside.

As Fargo waited for another target, he chuckled grimly to himself. At least he didn't have to worry about Mallory and the other outlaws anymore. They were all on the same side now, and they would be as long as they had to deal with the threat of the Indians.

Pete came up beside Fargo. "I got Mrs. Landon hunkered down behind the counter," he said.

"I saw that. Thanks."

"Looks like all the windows are covered. Reckon it's lucky Mallory and his bunch came along when they did." Pete wiped the back of a hand across his mouth and lowered his voice as he went on, "I figured we'd have trouble with them, sooner or later."

Fargo nodded. "So did I."

"But now we all need each other, I reckon." Pete sighed. "I knew my luck was bound to run out when it came to Injun trouble."

Fargo pointed out that actually he and Victoria were to blame for bringing down the war party on the trading post. "That wasn't our intention, though," he added.

Pete waved that off. "It don't matter none now. As long as we keep the varmints from gettin' in here, we'll be all right. I got plenty of food laid by, and the water barrel's full. It'll last a good while as long as we're careful with it."

"What about ammunition?"

"Got a lot of it, in several different calibers. We can stand 'em off, Fargo." Pete scratched his beard and grimaced worriedly. "That is, as long as them savages don't get the bright idea of tryin' to burn us out."

Fargo had started to worry about that, too. A few flaming arrows in the roof of the trading post would put them in a mighty bad position.

A fresh flurry of gunfire came from the other windows. One of Mallory's men called out, "Here they come!"

Fargo snapped the Henry to his shoulder and peered over the barrel as he thrust it out through the narrow opening between the shutters. He saw a buckskinned figure and fired. As the Crow warrior stumbled and fell, Fargo levered another round into the rifle's chamber and squeezed off a shot at the man who had taken the fallen warrior's place.

For the next thirty seconds or so, he was kept busy shooting. The time seemed much longer. A cloud of acrid powder-smoke filled the room, stinging the eyes and noses of everyone inside the trading post.

Fargo heard a crash from the bedroom. He hadn't seen the inside of the room, so he didn't know if there was a window in there or not. As Fargo wheeled in that direction, he saw Pete break into a run toward the door. "Damn it!" the trader yelled, and Fargo knew they had overlooked the possibility of a threat from that direction.

He just hoped it wouldn't turn out to be a fatal mistake.

The door opened before Pete got there. A Crow warrior charged through, rifle in hand. But before the Indian could fire, a savagely snarling Thor leaped at him, seemingly unhindered by having only three legs. The big dog's jaws closed over the warrior's right arm.

The Indian yelled in pain and staggered backward. Pete jammed the barrels of his shotgun into the Crow's midsection and pulled the triggers. The muffled boom was punctuated by the warrior's scream of agony as he was blown almost in half by the double charge of buckshot at point-blank range.

Fargo fired past the falling body at a second Indian who came through the bedroom door. The bullet from the Henry drilled into the Crow's forehead and sent him flying backward, dead before he hit the floor.

Mallory bounded past Pete and emptied his six-gun into the bedroom. The body of a third Crow warrior hit the floor. "Shoemaker, you and Tompkins get in there!" Mallory barked. "Cover that window they busted out!"

The two men rushed into the room; a second later a fusillade of shots sounded as they drove off more members of the war party, who were converging on the window.

Pete rubbed Thor behind the ears and said, "You're a mighty good dog, you mangy old cur. Yes, sir, you sure are."

Mallory reloaded his gun as he came over to Fargo. Scattered shots sounded from the men at the other windows. "We were damn lucky that time," Mallory said.

Fargo nodded. He had turned his attention back to the window he was covering. Without looking at Mallory, he said, "Pete thinks we've got enough food, water, and ammunition to hold them off for quite a while."

"Unless they decide to burn us out."

"That's what I'm worried about, too," Fargo admitted.

Mallory holstered his gun. "I been thinkin' about you, mister. That name of yours sounded familiar. Finally it came to me. You're the fella they call the Trailsman, ain't you?"

"Some have called me that," Fargo said.

"You've fought Indians a heap of times before now."

"I've been in my share of scrapes."

Mallory lowered his voice. "They say you can move as quiet as an Injun. It'll be dark in a little while. A man who really knew what he was doin' might be able to slip out of here and get away before those Crows knew what he was about."

Fargo glanced over at Mallory. "You think you could do that?"

"I don't know. But I ain't much of a mind to sit here and let those savages burn the place down around me."

"So you'd abandon the men you ride with." Fargo's voice was flat.

"Hell, there ain't a one of them who wouldn't do the same if he thought he could get away with it."

Fargo didn't say anything for a moment. Then he told Mallory, "Do whatever you want. I'm staying here."

Mallory's lips curled in a sneer under his drooping red mustache. "Could be you're a fool, Fargo."

"Could be I'd rather go down fighting than have those Crows capture me and torture me to death," Fargo shot back. "As long as I stay in here, I know *that* won't happen, anyway."

Mallory frowned and didn't say anything. Clearly, he was thinking about what Fargo had said. If he had spent much time on the frontier, he would know that death usually came long and hard for a man who was taken prisoner by hostile Indians.

"Reckon I'll stick around for a while," he finally said.

The shooting had gradually died away until an uneasy silence hung over the trading post and the area around it. No lamps had been lit inside the building, and the fireplace had died down to glowing embers, so the defenders could still see what was going on outside in the rapidly fading light.

While there was a lull in the fighting, Fargo asked Mallory to stay at the window he had been guarding. Mallory agreed with a touch of reluctance in his voice. Fargo made his way across the darkened room to the counter and went behind it.

He heard Victoria gasp. "Who—"

"It's me," he said. He hunkered on his heels, and guided by her voice, he put out a hand and found her shoulder. She reached up and caught hold of his arm. He asked, "Are you all right?"

"I . . . I suppose so. Just scared." She gave a hollow laugh. "It's almost like Fort Newcomb all over again. But not quite, because at least I'm not alone this time."

"That's right," Fargo told her as he gave her shoulder a squeeze. "We'll get out of this."

"I appreciate you saying that, Skye, but I know that we may not." She scooted closer to him on the floor. Her other hand rested on his chest. "The way I look at it, I should have died back there with Tom and the others. It was a miracle that I was spared. So everything that's happened since then . . . the time I've spent with you . . . that's been a miracle, too."

In the darkened room no one could see them, especially since they were behind the counter. Fargo drew her toward him. Their mouths met, tentatively at first because they could barely see each other, and then with more urgency and passion.

They couldn't make love under these circumstances but they could hold each other and draw strength from their closeness. That was exactly what they did for the next few minutes.

Then one of Mallory's men called softly, "I see somebody sneakin' around out there! Son of a bitch!" The man's voice rose. "They're settin' fire to some arrows!"

"Cut 'em down before they can shoot!" Mallory shouted.

Guns began to bang frantically as Fargo leaped up and raced out from behind the counter. He joined Mallory at the window as the man's revolver roared. It was almost completely dark outside now—a darkness lit up in garish fashion by flashcs from numerous gun muzzles.

Fargo and Mallory risked throwing the shutters wide open as they concentrated their shots on the flames visible from the burning arrows. Several of the arrows fell to the ground as the warriors who were about to send them flying toward the trading post were cut down by the scything lead.

But there were too many of them for Fargo, Mallory, and the other defenders to drop all of them. Several of the blazing arrows arched toward the log building. Fargo heard the impacts as they struck the roof.

Mallory grated a curse. "Now we're done for!"

"Maybe not," Pete said. "If we can get a couple of men with axes up in the rafters, they can chop a hole in the roof and we can throw water on the fire. The barrel's full."

That was their drinking water, Fargo thought, but

if the trading post burned down they wouldn't have to worry about dying of thirst. Pete's idea sounded like their only chance, so there was no time to waste.

"Keep shooting," he snapped at Mallory. "We have to keep the Indians from getting any more flaming arrows up there." He turned to Pete. "Where's an ax?"

"Come on," the trader said. He hurried over to the shelves and handed Fargo an ax from among the trade goods. He took up another for himself.

They ran to the counter and hoisted themselves onto it. Fargo was able to reach up and grab one of the rafters. He hauled himself up, then reached back down for the axes Pete handed up to him. Then he gave the trader a hand climbing into the open space between the rafters and the roof.

Fargo smelled smoke already. He glanced down and could barely make out Victoria's huddled shape behind the counter. Then he balanced himself on a rafter and started swinging the ax, chopping at the logs that made up the roof. It was an awkward position, but he put all the strength into it that he could. Beside him, Pete swung his own ax.

The firing continued below as Mallory and his men did their best to keep the situation from becoming even more desperate. A few more of the flaming arrows were fired at the trading post, then the Indians pulled back and hid in the brush along the riverbank once more.

Mallory yelled that news up to Fargo, who redoubled his efforts with the ax. The Crows wouldn't have pulled back if the fire on the roof wasn't spreading. Smoke drifted through cracks between the logs and made Fargo and Pete cough as they swung the axes.

Suddenly Fargo broke through the roof. He swung the ax harder, knocking off chunks of wood and making the hole larger.

"Get ready to pass some buckets of water up here!" Pete called down to the other men. Then he went back to work alongside Fargo, the two of them alternating blows with their axes.

Fargo saw the glow of the fire through the gap in the roof, but he couldn't see the flames themselves. After a couple of minutes, he thought the opening was large enough so that he could get his shoulders through it.

"Pass up the buckets!" he ordered as he tossed the ax aside and reached up to grasp the sides of the hole he and Pete had created.

Grunting with the effort, he hauled himself up until he was sitting on the edge of the hole. He saw immediately that three separate fires were burning on the roof—one to his left and two in front of him.

"Bucket!" Pete yelled.

Fargo reached down with one hand to grasp the water-filled bucket Pete held up toward him. As he lifted the bucket, he thought he heard yelling from the Indians. They had spotted him up here in the glow of the flames and figured out what he was trying to do.

He flung the water from the bucket onto the closest fire, then dropped the empty vessel back through the hole in the roof. Pete was waiting for it and caught it. An instant later, he had another full bucket in his hand that had been passed up to him by one of Mallory's men.

Fargo heard a wicked whine close to his ear and knew a bullet had just passed by him. A second later, an arrow—the regular kind, not a flaming one—struck the roof a couple of feet away. The feathered shaft quivered from the impact.

"Try to keep them busy!" he shouted as he sloshed the contents of the second bucket onto the flames.

The men who weren't engaged in the bucket brigade opened fire from the windows of the trading post, sending a storm of lead toward the war party. Fargo didn't really expect them to hit anything; he just wanted the Indians to be kept occupied dodging bullets, rather than trying to kill him. He was something of a sitting duck up here on the roof, lit up as it was by the fires.

For long minutes he worked at extinguishing the flames. The nearest fire was also the smallest one, and he got it put out fairly quickly. The other two blazes were more stubborn. The roof was wet now, however, so the flames didn't spread as fast.

A bullet chewed splinters from a log beside him, and he heard an arrow whistle past his head before it clattered off the roof. He paused long enough to draw his Colt and empty it toward the Indians' hiding places, thumbing off the shots as fast as he could. Then he jammed the revolver back in its holster and grabbed the next bucket of water.

The Crows tried again. Another flaming arrow sailed through the air and hit the roof to Fargo's right. He had splashed some water over there earlier, and the flames sputtered out without him even having to douse them. The other two fires were almost out now, too.

Fargo threw another couple of buckets full of water over the fires, and the last of the flames were extinguished. He dropped the bucket and slid down through the hole in the roof, hanging by his hands until he found a rafter with his feet.

"Keep them pinned down as much as you can!" he called to the defenders.

"You got all the fires out?" Pete asked.

Fargo nodded. "For now." He hoped he wouldn't have to go through that again. It had been harrowing up there on the roof.

Fargo and Pete swung back down and dropped onto the counter. Victoria stood up to greet Fargo as he climbed down to the floor. She hugged him and said, "I was sure those Indians would kill you, Skye."

He grinned. "They came pretty close a time or two. But you know the old saying about a miss being as good as a mile."

Only sporadic shots came from the defenders now. Smoky Jack Mallory walked over to Fargo and said, "Damn redskins are lyin' low. You could almost think they've decided to give up—that it's going to be too much trouble getting us out of here."

"I don't believe that," Fargo said with a shake of his head. "Broken Hand is too stubborn to give up that easily."

"I don't believe it, either," Mallory agreed. "But they're liable to wait a while before they come at us hard again."

"A little before dawn," Fargo said slowly. "I think that may be when they come calling again."

Everyone took advantage of the respite to eat and drink and rest a little, taking turns so that the windows were still guarded. Fargo sat behind the counter with Victoria for a while, the two of them talking quietly. Fargo became drowsy but fought off the feeling. No one could afford to sleep right now.

"I don't trust that man Mallory," Victoria said in a half-whisper. "He's on our side now, but only because of the danger from the Indians."

Fargo nodded. "Pete and I talked about the same thing. If we get out of this, we'll have to keep an eye on that bunch to make sure they don't try anything. They might not, though. Mallory's lost two men. The odds aren't quite as much in his favor."

And Mallory might lose more men before the siege was over, Fargo thought. But it didn't pay to dwell on such things when there was a much more immediate danger in the form of Broken Hand and the Crow war party.

The night passed slowly, the minutes and hours stretching out and drawing everyone's nerves taut. By the time the sky began to turn gray in the east with the approach of dawn, most of the defenders would have almost welcomed another attack by the Indians just to break the tension.

Fargo took the Henry and a couple of boxes of ammunition and told Victoria, Pete, and Two Bears, "I'm going back up on the roof. That's a good vantage point. If the Crows come at us again, I'll have good shots from up there."

"Yeah, but you'll be more exposed," Pete pointed out. "There ain't no cover."

"What about the chimneys? There's one at each end of the building."

Pete thought about it and said, "That's a dang good idea. I'll go up there with you."

Fargo wasn't sure he liked leaving Victoria in the trading post with Mallory and the other outlaws. But she wouldn't be completely alone. "Two Bears," Fargo said, "can you look after Mrs. Landon?"

The Shoshone nodded. "Two Bears watch over white missus."

"Skye . . ." Victoria began in worried tones. Fargo knew she wasn't fond of the idea of entrusting her safety to Two Bears. But then she stopped short and went on after a second. "You and Pete go ahead. Good luck to you both."

Fargo knew she was putting on a show of courage but he appreciated the gesture. And he trusted Two Bears. If Fargo asked it of him, the old Shoshone would die before he would let anyone hurt Victoria.

Pete armed himself with a Sharps rifle and a Colt, along with a good supply of ammunition for each, and then climbed onto the counter with Fargo. They clambered up into the rafters as they had before, taking guns with them this time instead of axes.

Fargo went through the hole in the roof first. Crouching low and hoping he wouldn't be seen, he hurried over to the chimney at the north end of the trading post. Pete took the other chimney. They hunkered beside the squarish stone columns, waiting.

When the rush came, it was sudden but not unexpected. Fargo saw movement in the gray shadows: a second later, a dozen Crow warriors charged forward. Behind them the rest of the war party opened fire with rifles and bows and arrows, concentrating their efforts on the windows.

Fargo understood the strategy. The window shutters were the weakest parts of the trading post. Broken Hand hoped the heavy barrage would make the defenders duck below the sills while the vanguard of the attackers charged across the open ground between the river and the building. If they reached the trading post, they would try to get inside; while that was going on, the rest of the war party would rush the place. It was a coordinated attack this time, rather than the haphazard carnage of the previous day and night.

But Fargo and Pete ruined the Indians' plan by opening fire from the roof. Fargo heard the boom of Pete's Sharps while his Henry cracked wickedly. Pete didn't take the time to reload the buffalo gun but began to blaze away with the Colt instead.

The slugs ripped through the warriors who were charging the cabin. Half of them went down and didn't get up again. Several others were wounded but stumbled on somehow. Only a couple of warriors weren't hit. Fargo lost sight of them as they came up to the building, but then gunfire roared from inside, and he was confident the Indians had been cut down.

The rest of the war party lifted their sights and began to rain lead and arrows on the roof. The chimney stuck out from the wall so that Fargo couldn't get completely behind it, but he crouched as low as he could at the very edge of the roof; rock chips and dust showered down on him from the bullets that struck it.

Fargo wondered how many of the war party had been killed, or wounded so badly that they were out of the fight. It had to be a considerable number. How long would Broken Hand keep up the attack? Was he blood thirsty enough that he would fight until the last warrior was dead?

The firing continued on both sides, sometimes furiously, sometimes only in sporadic bursts. Broken Hand's main thrust had been blunted. Now he would have to come up with something else.

As the sun rose, Fargo realized that he and Pete had stayed on the roof too long. Now they couldn't get back to the hole in the center without exposing themselves to the Crows' fire. He looked over at Pete, who shrugged, evidently having the same thought. They would just have to wait it out.

Not for long, it turned out because hoofbeats suddenly rattled along the river bank. Fargo risked a look and saw the Indians riding away hurriedly to the south.

"What the hell?" Pete called over to him, having seen the same thing.

"Looks like they're pulling out," Fargo replied. He suspected a trick, but as he estimated the number of riders galloping away from the trading post, he thought it had to be most, if not all, of the war party.

Had Broken Hand finally given up his quest for vengeance? It seemed hard to believe, but Fargo couldn't come up with any other answer.

Then, stiffening, he saw the reason for their abrupt departure as he looked across at the heights on the other side of the Missouri River. Riders had appeared there—scores of riders in buckskins and feathered headdresses. More and more of them moved into sight and pulled their mounts to a halt so that they sat there motionless, etched against the red sky of dawn.

Fargo wished he had some field glasses so he could tell for sure, but he was convinced that these newcomers were Blackfeet, the sworn enemies of the Crows. The war party was huge, growing to well over a hundred strong as Fargo watched.

"Oh, Lord," Pete said hollowly. "Look at 'em just a-sittin' over there. Fargo, we're really in trouble now."

"Maybe," Fargo said. "Maybe not."

He looked to the south. Broken Hand and the other Crows were out of sight now. Outnumbered by more than four to one, they had done the sensible thing and fled, though it had probably galled them considerably to do so. Especially Broken Hand. His failure to catch the people he had pursued had to be a blow to his pride, not to mention to his standing with the other warriors. Staying to fight the Blackfeet, though, would have accomplished nothing except to get his whole group wiped out.

Silence reigned as Fargo and Pete watched the large band of Blackfeet on the other side of the river. Finally, Mallory yelled from inside, "What the hell's goin' on up there?"

Across the Missouri, the Blackfeet turned their horses and started riding slowly south. Their pace increased as one by one they vanished over a ridge.

Fargo filled his lungs with air, unaware until that moment that he had been holding his breath. "It's all right," he called down through the hole in the roof. "We're safe now. Broken Hand and his warriors are gone." He could explain why the Crows had taken off for the tall and uncut after he was back inside the trading post, he decided.

He wondered if the Blackfeet would try to catch up

to Broken Hand's war party. It seemed likely, given the state of hostilities between the tribes. Broken Hand would probably regret chasing Fargo and Victoria up here, if he didn't already.

Fargo didn't mind that a bit.

He straightened from his crouch and started toward the hole in the roof. Pete came over from the chimney at the other end of the building.

They had almost reached the hole when a pair of gunshots rang out inside the trading post and Victoria Landon let out a frightened scream.

6

"Fargo!" Smoky Jack Mallory shouted. "Fargo, you hear me?"

Fargo stood tensely on the roof, facing the hole. Mallory hadn't wasted any time making his move once the danger from the Indians appeared to be over.

"I hear you!"

"What happened? Where'd those Indians go?"

"First tell me what happened down there!" Fargo demanded. "I heard Mrs. Landon scream."

Mallory laughed. "The lady's just fine. Tell Fargo you're all right, Mrs. Landon."

"Skye!" Victoria cried. "He shot Two Bears! He—"

Her voice was muffled and cut off abruptly by what sounded like a hand being clapped over her mouth. Fargo's jaw tightened even more as anger welled up inside him.

He saw Pete take a step toward the hole and motioned for the trader to stay back. As long as they didn't get too close to the opening in the roof, the outlaws inside the trading post couldn't see them to shoot at them. Fargo figured Mallory and his men would take the first opportunity to kill them.

"You heard for yourself that she's all right, Fargo," Mallory shouted. "Now tell me what I want to know—and by God you'd better not lie!"

"The Crows left because an even bigger war party of Blackfeet showed up on the other side of the river." Fargo tried a bluff. "In fact, they're still over there, so you'd better call off whatever you think you're doing, Mallory. We're going to have to be fighting on the same side again in a few minutes."

He heard muttered cursing, then Mallory snapped, "Gramlich, get out there and take a look. See if those Blackfeet are still over there."

Fargo heard the door of the trading post open. A moment later, the outlaw called back, "I don't see a thing, Jack. No Blackfeet over there across the river."

"Damn you, Fargo, I told you not to lie," Mallory said.

Fargo didn't know what Mallory would do, but he spoke quickly to keep the man from taking out his anger on Victoria. "Gramlich can't see them from where he is. They're back a quarter of a mile or so from the bank. But they're there, aren't they, Pete?"

"They sure are," Pete chimed in, nodding to Fargo that he understood the bluff. "You better call a truce, Mallory."

There was silence from below while Mallory evidently thought it over. Fargo was worried about Two Bears and wanted to check on the old Shoshone. Victoria had said that Mallory shot him. Two Bears had already been wounded once by the outlaw leader. Maybe now his luck had run out.

"You still don't see anything?" Mallory called to his man at the door.

"Not a damned thing, Jack!"

"Well, go out farther and take a look around. Shoemaker, you go with him."

That order brought a worried protest from the man at the door. "Jack, are you sure that's a good idea? There could be some of those redskins still lurkin' around—"

"Do what I said, damn it!" Mallory roared. "Or you'll get what this redskin in here got!"

Fargo heard the two outlaws walk outside, and he knew that the bluff wasn't going to work. That meant he and Pete would have to seize the only opportunity they had. He put down his rifle and motioned toward the front of the building. Pete nodded.

They moved fast, and as they reached the edge of the roof, Fargo saw that his guess was correct: the two men on the ground were more worried about Blackfeet than they were the threat from above. Fargo launched himself into the air, diving toward the man on the left. Pete aimed for the one on the right.

The outlaws saw them coming, but not in time to do anything other than bleat out alarmed yells. Fargo had drawn his Colt as he made his dive. He slammed the gun barrel against Gramlich's skull as he crashed into him and drove him to the ground.

The outlaw broke his fall, and the blow from Fargo's gun knocked the man cold. Fargo was able to scramble back to his feet right away. As he swung around, he saw that Pete was having a harder time of it with Shoemaker. Not only that, but the door of the trading post was open and Mallory had seen what was going on.

"Kill them!" Mallory shouted. "Kill them both!"

The outlaws crowded the doorway, guns in hands, but they hesitated to shoot because their two companions were in the line of fire. That gave Fargo time to thumb off a couple of rounds. The bullets chewed splinters off the doorjamb and sent the owlhoots ducking back frantically.

Pete had managed to get on top of Shoemaker. He wrapped his hands around the outlaw's neck and slammed his head against the ground a couple of times. Stunned, the man went limp underneath him.

Fargo grabbed Gramlich and dragged him off to one

side. Pete went the other way with his man. They hauled their unconscious burdens up next to the wall on either side of the door, away from the windows.

"Mallory!" Fargo called. "Now we have hostages, too! Send Mrs. Landon out unharmed or we'll kill your men."

Mallory laughed coldly from inside the trading post. "Go ahead and kill the dumb bastards! If they're stupid enough to get themselves caught, it's what they deserve!"

Fargo and Pete exchanged glances. It was hard to deal with a man as callous and brutal as Mallory. Fargo didn't know if he meant what he said about killing the two men, but there was no way Fargo was going to murder them in cold blood. Mallory was probably counting on that.

Besides, if the captives were dead, Fargo and Pete wouldn't have any bargaining chips at all.

"There's no need for us to fight, Mallory," Fargo said as he leaned against the wall, Colt drawn. "We fought those Crows together. That ought to count for something. You go your way, and we'll go ours."

Again that cold laugh came from Mallory. "You can leave any time you want, Fargo . . . but the woman goes with us."

"No deal," Fargo said flatly.

"How do you know she don't *want* to go with us? Maybe we'll treat her better than you ever could."

By raping her until she was half-dead and then slitting her throat to finish the job? Fargo didn't think so. He didn't know if the Indians had left them any horses or not, but he knew he wasn't riding away from here and leaving Victoria with the outlaws.

He stalled for time by saying, "I'd have to hear Mrs. Landon tell me that herself."

"Well, hell, maybe we can arrange that." The sharp crack of a hand against flesh came from inside the cabin. "Tell him, woman," Mallory commanded. "Tell him you want to go with us."

Fargo was filled with such rage at the sound of Victoria being slapped that he could barely restrain himself from leaping into the doorway and blazing away with the Colt. That would be a good way to get her killed, though, so he managed to rein in his temper.

After a moment, Victoria said in a weak voice, "Skye . . . ?"

"I'm here," he called to her.

"Skye, I want you to . . . to . . ." Her voice suddenly strengthened. "To kill this son of a bitch the first chance you get!"

Mallory roared a curse and hit her again. Fargo heard the sound of the blow and clenched his jaw firmly as he held himself back.

"All right!" Mallory said. "That don't change nothin'! She's still goin' with us. In fact, we're comin' out right now, and my gun's at her head. You try anything and I'll splatter her brains all over the place, Fargo!"

Fargo heard the scrape of boot leather on the trading post's puncheon floor as someone approached the door. As he expected, Mallory came out first, bringing Victoria with him. The outlaw's left arm was looped around her long, slender neck, and he had the barrel of his gun jammed against the side of her head, just above her right ear.

Fargo could tell from the expression on Victoria's face that she was in pain. She was also having trouble breathing because Mallory's arm was pressed so tightly across her throat.

"Back off, Fargo," Mallory grated. "Back off, or I swear I'll kill the woman."

Fargo had his gun trained on the outlaw leader. "If you kill her, there's nothing to stop me from killing you," he pointed out.

An ugly grin stretched across Mallory's bearded face. "No, but you'd have to watch her die first, and I'm willin' to bet you won't do that."

He was right, of course. Fargo couldn't let him shoot Victoria. As long as she was alive, there was still a chance that Fargo could rescue her from the outlaws.

Mallory's eyes flicked toward Pete. "You," he said. "Get our horses."

Pete looked at Fargo, who gave a curt nod. With a scowl at Mallory, Pete tucked the revolver into his belt behind him and started for the corral.

Fargo didn't think the Indians had stolen the horses, and sure enough Pete came back a few tense minutes later leading several of the mounts. "I'll have to go back for the others," he said.

By this time, Mallory had moved out about a dozen feet from the door, and the rest of the gang had joined him, except for the one killed in the first attack who had made it inside before dying. The other dead outlaw lay over by the other corner of the trading post, peppered with arrows.

The bodies of several dead Crow warriors lay scattered in front of the trading post, too. When a battle was over, Indians liked to take the bodies of the men who had been killed with them, but in this case Broken Hand hadn't been able to recover all of his men.

Without taking the gun away from Victoria's head, Mallory ordered his men to pick up Gamlich and Shoemaker, who had been jumped and knocked out by Fargo and Pete. Those outlaws were stirring around and beginning to show signs of returning consciousness. Their companions lifted them onto their feet.

Fargo kept his gun pointed at Mallory. He fully expected the gang leader to order the others to kill Fargo and Pete before they rode away from the trading post. Mallory wasn't the sort of man to leave an enemy behind who might come after him.

If it came down to that, Fargo wouldn't just stand there and let the outlaws murder him. He would fight back and would take as many of them with him as he could. He just hoped one of them would be Smoky Jack Mallory.

Pete brought the rest of the horses around the building. He still had hold of the reins when a bloody figure suddenly stumbled out of the trading post. Two Bears had a gun in his hand, and without warning, the old Shoshone brought the weapon up and shot one of the outlaws in the back.

The blast flung the man forward. Before he hit the ground, Two Bears was already swinging the Colt to bring it in line with another of the outlaws. The gun roared again. The bullet ripped into the side of a man who was trying to turn toward the old Indian.

Fargo hadn't been expecting the distraction, but he reacted instantly to it. As Mallory swung around to see what the shooting was about, Fargo fired a carefully aimed shot. The bullet tore across the outside of Mallory's upper right arm, knocking him halfway around.

Mallory jerked the trigger, but he was too late. He had already pulled the gun barrel away from Victoria's head.

She kicked at him and tried to pull free from his grip. Mallory bellowed a curse and dragged her closer to him, using her as a shield. His right arm hung useless at his side, but he managed not to drop his gun.

Seeing that he didn't have another shot at Mallory, Fargo wheeled toward the other men just as Pete yelled and jerked off his hat. The trader slapped the headgear against the rumps of the horses and sent the spooked animals plunging toward the outlaws. The group in front of the door became a confused tangle of men and horses.

A bullet whistled past Fargo's head. He fired back and saw one of the outlaws go spinning off his feet.

Another man went down, knocked to the ground by one of the horses. He screamed for a second as its iron-shod hooves trampled him, then abruptly fell silent as his skull was crushed by one of the blows.

Fargo lost track of Mallory and Victoria in the melee. He rushed forward, looking for them. One of the outlaws loomed in front of him, face twisted with hate and rage. The man tried to bring his gun to bear, but he was too quick on the trigger. The bullet plucked at a piece of fringe on the Trailsman's buckskin shirt, and then Fargo fired from the hip. The man doubled over as a slug bored through his guts.

"Skye!" Victoria screamed.

Fargo twisted toward the sound of that cry and saw that Mallory had flung her across the back of one of the horses. Awkwardly, because of his wounded arm, Mallory vaulted into the saddle and kicked the horse into a run.

The Trailsman snapped a shot at him, but at that moment, Mallory leaned forward over the neck of the horse, using his weight to help hold down the struggling Victoria. The bullet whined harmlessly a foot over his head.

Fargo would have grabbed a horse and gone after them, but something struck him a tremendous blow on the side of the head. A bright red explosion seemed to fill his skull, and although he knew he was falling, there was nothing he could do about it.

By the time he hit the ground, the red had been replaced by an all-engulfing black.

Pain radiated through Fargo's body. That was the first thing he was aware of as consciousness seeped back into his brain. In a way, he welcomed the pain, because he knew it meant he wasn't dead.

Once that was settled in his mind, his iron will was able to shove the pain off into a corner of his brain where he could ignore it. He pried his eyes open and found himself looking up into the weathered face of Poudre River Pete.

"Dadgum!" Pete exclaimed. "You're awake. I knew you was still alive, Fargo, but I was afraid you'd die without ever wakin' up again."

Fargo tried to move his head to look around and see where he was, but that made the world start spinning crazily. He lay as still as possible, breathing shallowly, until the feeling passed and the sickness that cramped his belly eased. He looked at Pete again and said hoarsely, "Victoria . . . ?"

Pete shook his head. "That bastard Mallory got away with her. None of the others made it, though. They're all dead."

"What about . . . Two Bears?"

"He's alive."

Fargo closed his eyes for a second and sighed with relief.

"That Injun's a tough old bird," Pete went on. "He says Mallory threw down on him once you yelled that about the Crows bein' gone. Shot him twice and thought he was dead. But he wasn't. He passed out for a spell, but when he came to, he got up, found a gun, and took a hand in that standoff. Lucky for us he did, too."

Fargo was able to nod without getting dizzy or sick this time. He licked his dry lips and asked, "How bad am I hit?"

"Looks like a bullet just barely grazed your head, but that was enough to knock you out for a while. It bled a heap, so I thought it was worse'n it really was. I got you and Two Bears back inside and tried to patch up both of you as best I could."

Fargo heard the shuffle of feet, and then Two Bears said, "Pete did good job."

Fargo raised himself on an elbow and saw that he

was lying on a pallet on the floor, near the fireplace. Pete hunkered next to him and Two Bears stood to one side. The Shoshone's left arm was in a sling, and his buckskin shirt had been replaced by bandages wrapped tightly around his torso.

Pete grinned. "Two Bears is a lucky fella. One slug grazed his ribs and maybe cracked one of them, and the other took a chunk of meat out of his arm but missed the bone. He's one shot-up Injun, but I reckon with a little luck he'll be all right."

Fargo raised a hand to his head and felt the bandage Pete had tied around it. He winced as he touched the tender welt the bullet had left above his ear.

"I've got to get up," he said as he started trying to climb to his feet. "I've got to go after Mallory—"

Again a wave of dizziness washed over him, and he would have fallen if Pete had not grabbed his arm to steady him.

"Hold on there," the trader said. "I'm as worried about Miz Landon as you are, Fargo, but you ain't in no shape to go gallivantin' over the countryside. You've got to rest and let your head settle down."

"Can't," Fargo muttered stubbornly. "Told her I'd . . . protect her. . . ."

But even as he spoke, he felt himself about to pass out again. This time when Pete urged him to lie down, he didn't argue. His eyes closed of their own volition, as if each eyelid weighed a hundred pounds.

When he regained consciousness, it was more like he was waking up from a natural sleep. His head still hurt, but the throbbing was bearable. He was able to sit up without too much trouble, and when he did, he saw Pete and Two Bears sitting at the rough-hewn table. The smell of stew filled the air, and—somewhat to Fargo's amazement—he found that he was hungry.

Pete got up and came over to help him to his feet.

"You look a mite better," he said. "Reckon you ain't ready for the grave after all."

Fargo sat down carefully in one of the empty chairs. "What time is it?" he asked.

"Nearly nightfall. You been out pretty much all day."

Fargo bit back a curse. That meant Mallory had a long head start on him. Anything could have happened to Victoria by now—and probably had.

"Is my horse all right?"

"Yeah, that big fella's fine."

Fargo nodded. He didn't think the Crows could have captured the Ovaro, but with all the fighting that had gone on, the stallion might have been hit by a wild bullet or an arrow. It was a relief to know that the big black-and-white horse was unharmed.

"I'll get him saddled up—"

"Whoa there," Pete said. "It'll be dark in less'n half an hour. You can't trail Mallory at night."

"I can't let him get more of a lead on me," Fargo insisted.

"Likely he'll stop for the night, too. You can get on his trail first thing in the morning if you feel up to it."

"I'll feel up to it," Fargo declared grimly. He had no choice in the matter.

But Pete was right: not even the Trailsman could track his quarry at night.

Pete dished up a bowl of stew for Fargo and filled his cup with coffee. The food made Fargo feel better. He knew, though, that he was not yet back to full strength.

"Mallory was headed downstream when he left here," Fargo mused over a second cup of coffee. "I wonder if he'll keep going in that direction."

"That's the only thing that makes sense for him to do," Pete said. "With winter comin' on, and especially without his gang to back him up no more, he'll head for Fort Benton." The trader scratched his beard. "Don't know what he'll do about Miz Landon, though. When they get there she's liable to tell the army about what he done."

Fargo shook his head. "She won't ever get there. Mallory will kill her." His hope was that the outlaw leader would keep Victoria alive until he was closer to the fort. That would give Fargo a chance to catch up to them.

"That Mallory is bad man," Two Bears said. "He shoot Two Bears for no reason."

Pete nodded. "Yeah, the old-timer told me about that," he said to Fargo. "What kind of fella hauls off and shoots a stranger for no reason at all?"

"An evil one," Fargo said.

The sort that needed to be put down like a mad dog. . . .

Fargo woke up the next morning with a dog that definitely wasn't mad licking his face.

"Thor, get away from there, dadgummit!" Pete said. "Leave ol' Fargo alone."

Fargo was stretched out on the pallet in front of the fire. He threw off the bearskin robe he had used for a blanket and sat up. The pain in his head had receded to a dull, easily ignored ache.

Even after being asleep most of the previous day, he had slept soundly during the night. His muscles were a little stiff as he got to his feet, but other than that, hc fclt pretty good. He reached down and scratched Thor behind the ears.

Pete had bacon and biscuits cooking in a skillet over the fire. Two Bears sat at the table. Fargo went outside to have a look around and found the sky overcast, with an icy wind blowing out of the north. He frowned. If a storm came in and it started to snow, that would cover up any tracks that Mallory had left.

He walked behind the trading post to the corral. The Ovaro greeted him with a whinny and a toss of the head. The stallion seemed to be in fine shape, ready to run.

That was good, Fargo thought. He would have to move fast if he was going to catch up to Mallory and Victoria. The outlaw's horse would be carrying double, which meant Mallory would have to go slower. Also, Mallory wouldn't know if Fargo was even still alive, let alone coming after him. After a while with no signs of pursuit, the natural thing would be for Mallory to take it a little easier.

Fargo counted on those two things to give him an edge . . . an edge he would need if he was going to save Victoria's life.

"What happened to all the bodies?" he asked Pete when he went back inside.

"I chucked 'em off the bluff into the river." Pete held up a hand, palm out. "I know, I know, it was a mighty hard-hearted thing to do. But every one of those boys, white and red alike, tried to kill me at one time or another in the past twenty-four hours, and I just didn't feel like diggin' graves for 'em. Besides, I had my hands full takin' care of you and Two Bears."

Fargo nodded and said, "You don't hear me complaining." Under normal circumstances, he preferred to give anyone a decent burial, even his enemies. But these circumstances were far from normal.

Breakfast was ready. Fargo ate with a hearty appetite and drank several cups of coffee. When he was finished, he said, "I need some ammunition and supplies, and then I'll hit the trail."

"Just tell me what you want and I'll get it for you."

Pete studied Fargo through narrowed eyes. "You sure you're all right to travel?"

"I'm fine," Fargo said with a nod. It was true. His head didn't even hurt anymore. His hardy constitution and the rugged life he'd led had given him the ability to shrug off most minor injuries.

While Pete packed up some food and boxes of cartridges for the Henry and the Colt, Fargo said to Two Bears, "I reckon you'll stay here for the winter."

The old Shoshone nodded. "Pete has already agreed. I would go with you, my friend, but as Pete says, Two Bears is one shot-up Injun."

Fargo squeezed his shoulder and grinned. "You already saved Mrs. Landon's life, and probably mine, too. As far as I'm concerned, we're square. You stay here and rest and get over those wounds, and I hope our trails cross again someday."

"This is Two Bears' hope as well," the old man agreed solemnly.

Fargo was ready to ride. He saddled up the Ovaro, fastened the full saddlebags over the stallion's back, and led him around to the front of the trading post.

Pete and Two Bears stood outside the door to say their farewells. Thor sat beside Pete, tongue lolling out.

Fargo swung up onto the saddle. Pete raised a hand and called, "Good luck!"

"Thanks. You fellas take it easy."

There was nothing else to say. Fargo waved goodbye as he turned the Ovaro and heeled the big horse into an easy lope. He rode off in the same direction Mallory had gone with Victoria. Already, his eyes were scanning the ground for tracks.

The wind was still cold, the sky gray and forbidding. The weather basically matched his mood, Fargo thought. He had to force himself not to dwell on what Victoria might be going through at that very moment.

One thing was certain, Fargo told himself. Sooner or later, he would have his showdown with Smoky Jack Mallory. And when that day came, only one of them would walk away.

7

Mallory hadn't been trying to conceal his trail when he galloped away from the trading post with Victoria screaming and struggling in front of him. Fargo had no trouble following them.

Several miles downriver, he came to a spot where the tracks and a day-old pile of horse droppings indicated that Mallory had stopped for a short time. Fargo figured Mallory had come this far at a gallop, then decided it was safe to rein in and get Victoria mounted in a more traditional fashion. A couple of her footprints, with the heels of her shoes dug in deeply, marked the spot where she had slid down from the horse.

Fargo frowned as he looked at more of her footprints. They were farther apart than a normal walking stride. She had tried to run when Mallory let her down. But she hadn't gotten far before her captor tackled her. Fargo read that story plain as day from the way the sparse grass was trampled down.

He hoped Mallory hadn't raped her right then and there. It was unlikely. No matter how much of a lustful brute Mallory was, he had known that a fierce gunfight was going on only a few miles back upriver and that Fargo might soon be coming after him. Mallory would have forced Victoria back onto the horse and ridden on, putting more distance between them and the trading post.

When Mallory had moved on again, he no longer galloped his horse wildly. Fargo had expected him to slow down, and was glad to see that his guess was right. It was a mixed blessing: By going slower, Mallory hadn't gotten as far ahead as he might have otherwise, but he had also been more careful not to leave such an easy-to-follow trail.

Still, Fargo was able to track his quarry. He saw every crushed blade of grass, every nick on a rock left by a horseshoe, every broken branch. That ability came naturally to him, and long years of practice had made his senses even keener.

From time to time, he glanced up at the sky. The clouds didn't break, but there was no snow yet. The longer the storm held off, the better.

All that morning, Fargo tracked Mallory and Victoria. The terrain was rugged. The Big Belt Range rose across the river to the east; to the west was the main body of the Rockies, known in this area as the Lewis Range, after Meriwether Lewis. The peaks pinched in loomingly toward the Missouri on both sides.

He came to a spot where Mallory had stopped again for what seemed to be a longer time. There were even the remains of a small campfire. They hadn't spent the night, though. There weren't enough horse droppings for that.

Fargo followed the trail onward as the river began to curve slightly to the northeast. It would continue that gradual curve until it was running almost due east across the plains before starting its southeastward bend toward its ultimate rendezvous with the Mississippi.

He would catch up to Mallory and Victoria long before that, however. He had to if he wanted to have any chance of saving Victoria's life.

During the afternoon, the skin on the back of Fargo's neck began to crawl. He knew what that meant: Someone was watching him.

Without being too obvious about it, he checked his back-trail but didn't see anything. That told him whoever was following him was good at it. He kept moving, not letting on that he was aware someone was on his trail.

By late afternoon, he was convinced he had cut into the lead that Mallory and Victoria had on him. He debated whether he ought to continue riding after night fell. That would mean he'd have to assume that Mallory would continue to follow the river, but really, where else could the man go? Fort Benton was the closest outpost of civilization, and with the weather worsening, Mallory would have no choice but to head there. Fargo decided to take a chance and push on, at least for a while.

He knew he was gambling with Victoria's life. But if his hunch was correct, he felt confident that he could catch up to them sometime the next day.

The wind grew colder as darkness settled on the land. Fargo huddled in his sheepskin coat as he kept his horse moving at a quick and steady pace. He had stopped several times during the day to give the big stallion a brief rest, so the Ovaro was still strong. Even such a magnificent animal had its limits, though.

As for Fargo himself, the day's ride, coupled with the injury he had suffered during the battle at the trading post, had worn him out. But he had reserves of strength and knew he could keep going. There would be time enough for a long rest when Victoria was safely out of Mallory's clutches.

The sound of the river gushing through its channel to his right guided him. The night was so dark he couldn't see very far in front of him. After a while, tiny bits of wetness began to spit against his face.

Snow.

Fargo bit back a curse. It was a good thing he had decided to keep moving. The weather was going to force him to forget about tracking and just head for Fort Benton as fast as he could. Now he was just going to have to trust to luck that he would catch up to Mallory and Victoria before they got there.

Maybe the storm wouldn't be too bad. A light snowfall would be manageable. But if this was one of those early blizzards that sometimes struck with unexpected ferocity, likely he would freeze to death before it was over, unless he could find a cave or some other sort of shelter.

For now he would keep moving.

The snow fell thicker and the wind grew stronger. A normal man's spirits would have drooped, but Fargo's nature would not allow that. He pushed on, dimly aware of the river valley narrowing and the mountains looming up closer on both sides of the waterway. The terrain acted as a funnel, directing the savage wind right into his face.

The Ovaro would have kept going as long as Fargo asked him to. Fargo knew that. He also knew he had to find some place to get out of this storm, or he and the horse would both be dead by morning.

Fargo turned the stallion's head to the left, veering away from the river. He found himself in a wasteland of boulders and steep, rocky bluffs. When the wind suddenly slackened a little, he reined in. He swung down from the saddle and then walked forward, one hand out in front of him while the other grasped the reins. As his fingers touched rock, the force of the wind lessened even more.

Fargo reached into his coat, found a lucifer in his shirt pocket, and bent over it as he snapped the match to life with his thumbnail. Blocking the wind with his body as best he could, he looked around in the brief flare, before the flame was sucked out.

He was at the mouth of an open space between a couple of bluffs that leaned together. It wasn't really a cave, but it was the next best thing. Fargo pushed deeper into the area between the looming slabs of rock. The bluff to the north completely blocked the wind. Fargo felt warmer already.

Knowing the Ovaro wouldn't go anywhere, he dropped the stallion's reins and began feeling around for wood to make a fire. He found a few branches and a little dried brush that had blown in, and within minutes he had a small fire going, the red and gold flames dancing merrily. The rocks reflected the welcome heat.

Fargo unsaddled the horse and gave him a little grain. Then he sat down with his back against one of the rock walls and took some jerky and a biscuit from one of his saddlebags.

The area where he had taken refuge was about twelve feet wide at its base and maybe forty feet long. The bluffs came together some twenty feet over his head. He couldn't have asked for a much better shelter. The area being open at both ends meant that an occasional gust of wind blew through there, but nothing like what was going on outside, where the wind howled viciously.

As he ate his supper, Fargo thought about whoever had been following him earlier in the day. Had they gone to ground somewhere, too? If they hadn't, they would probably freeze to death in the storm, plunge blindly into a ravine, or meet their end in some other unpleasant manner.

Not that there was really a *pleasant* way to die, Fargo mused. He had always lived life to the fullest, the best he knew how, and he wasn't afraid of what lay on the other side. But there were trails he hadn't yet ridden, mountains he hadn't yet climbed, sunsets he hadn't watched in all their glory. He still had so much to do. . . .

But that was true of every man when he came to the end, wasn't it?

With a little shake of his head, Fargo pushed that thought away. He had other things with which to concern himself. Where were Mallory and Victoria tonight? Had they found shelter from the storm?

The sudden pricking of the Ovaro's ears as he raised his head alerted Fargo. That moment of warning was enough to let him reach for his Colt before two yelling figures charged him, one from each end of the cave-like area.

Fargo went over the little fire in a rolling dive as guns blasted and bullets whined off the rock wall where he had been leaning a second earlier. He came up in a crouch with the Colt in his hand and triggered the revolver at the nearer of the two attackers. A couple of slugs bored into the Indian's chest and smashed him backward.

But that gave the second man time to reach Fargo and swing the empty single-shot rifle in his hands like a club. Fargo ducked desperately to avoid the blow. Out of control from his momentum, the second Indian crashed into Fargo. The collision sent both men sprawling on the ground.

Fargo managed to hang on to his gun. As he rolled over, he saw yet another Indian lunging at him, tomahawk in hand. He thrust the revolver up as the tomahawk swooped down, using the Colt to block the blow. At the same time, Fargo snapped a kick into the third Indian's belly.

The second attacker was back up by now and again swung his rifle like a club. Fargo rolled aside just in time to avoid the blow. The rifle's stock shattered against the hard ground. Already off-balance, the Indian fell as Fargo's leg swept his feet out from under him.

Fargo leaped up as the third man recovered from the kick and came at him again. For the first time in the flurry of life-and-death action, Fargo got a look at the decorations on the man's buckskins and recognized them as Crow.

The last he had seen of Broken Hand's warriors, they had been hotfooting it out of the area with a Blackfoot war party on their tail. Maybe these men were from a different bunch of Crow, or maybe some of Broken Hand's men had gotten away, circled around somehow, and continued their pursuit of Fargo. All that really mattered at the moment was that they wanted to kill him.

He jumped out of the way of a couple of slashing blows from the tomahawk. He could have shot the Indian, but he held off. If he could capture one or both of the remaining Crows, maybe he could find out whether they were Broken Hand's men.

Fargo backed up against the wall and leveled the Colt at the two men. The second one still clutched the barrel of the broken rifle and could wield it as a deadly weapon.

Fargo didn't know if they spoke any English. He commanded them in the Crow tongue to drop their weapons.

Instead, with snarling, hate-filled faces, they sprang at him again.

He had no choice. Flame bloomed as the heavy revolver spat death. The shots echoed off the rock walls in a deafening roll of thunder. Both of Fargo's attackers were flung backwards by the bullets that slammed into their bodies. They fell limply to the ground, dropping their weapons at last.

Fargo felt a little sick. He knew he could have tried to wound them, but he also knew that wouldn't have stopped them. They would have kept coming at him as long as breath remained in their bodies. His hard-featured face didn't reveal what he really felt as he reloaded the empty chambers of his gun.

"Fargo!"

The shout made his head jerk up and his lips pull back from his teeth in a grimace. It came from outside, but the storm and the wind made it difficult to tell exactly where the voice originated.

"Fargo, you hear me?"

The voice belonged to a man, but it wasn't one that Fargo knew. He stepped quickly to the fire and kicked out the flames so that darkness filled the cleft in the rocks.

"I know you hear me, Fargo! I could have shot you, but I wanted you to know who will be responsible for your death! My name is Broken Hand!"

The Crow war chief spoke English quite well, probably having learned the language at some mission school.

"My men rushed in when they should not have!" Broken Hand went on, shouting above the wind. "They were too eager to spill your blood! Now you have killed them, and I am alone! But I will still be your death, Fargo! I will come for you, and your life will be mine! My hands will spill your blood! Watch for me, though you will not see me until it is too late!" He laughed, the sound fading away into a last faint call. "Watch for your death, Fargo. . . ."

For long minutes, Fargo stood motionless, his back pressed to the rock. He knew Broken Hand might be trying to trick him. Even now, the war chief might be slipping up to the cleft's entrance to try to kill him.

But there was no sound in the darkness except for the wind, and finally Fargo's instincts told him that Broken Hand was gone.

For now.

* * *

Fargo didn't rekindle the fire after dragging the bodies of the dead Indians outside. He didn't want to make himself a target, just in case Broken Hand was still lurking somewhere nearby.

As the Crow war chief had pointed out, however, he could have already shot Fargo from ambush if that was what he wanted. From what Broken Hand had said, he wanted to kill Fargo in hand-to-hand combat. That was the only way his damaged honor would truly be satisfied.

The night was long and cold. Fargo wrapped himself in his blankets and slept fitfully, relying as before on the big stallion to alert him if anyone else came near.

In the morning, when he came out of the little cave-like area between the two leaning bluffs, he saw that the snow hadn't been too heavy. There were deep drifts in places, but the hard wind had scoured the snow off the flatter sections of ground.

As Fargo expected, the bodies were gone, more than likely dragged off by wolves.

The sky was still overcast, but the wind had died down to almost nothing. An eerie quiet hung over the world. Fargo saddled the Ovaro and mounted up. He chewed on a strip of jerky as he rode and let that do for breakfast.

He vividly remembered Broken Hand's warning and was sure the Crow was still somewhere close by. Fargo watched constantly for any sign of an ambush, and whenever possible he avoided places where Broken Hand might be lying in wait.

But he couldn't afford to be so careful that it slowed him down. He still had to cover ground as quickly as possible so he could catch up to Mallory. The knowledge that Victoria might already be dead was like a bitter taste in the back of his throat.

The bluffs flanking the river grew even taller and steeper, forming sheer limestone cliffs that towered a thousand feet or more above the Missouri. By this point, the river stretched fifty yards wide in most places. It twisted and turned like a snake, seldom running more than a quarter of a mile without a bend. This was some of the most spectacular country in the West—even under overcast, wintry skies—and if he had not been so worried about Victoria, Fargo would have enjoyed the sight.

It was nearing the middle of the day when Fargo spotted movement on the far side of the river. He reined in and looked across the swiftly flowing water, to where another horseman had halted to look at him. The Trailsman's hawklike eyes saw the buckskins and the feathers fastened in the thick black hair.

The Indian sat and watched Fargo for a moment, then wheeled his pony and rode away in an unhurried fashion. Fargo was pretty sure the man hadn't been Broken Hand. He knew the Crow war chief was on this side of the river, and there were no fords in the vicinity. The closest ford, Fargo knew, was on the other side of the Great Falls of the Missouri. More than likely, the Indian had been a Blackfoot.

Fargo didn't know what the encounter might mean, if anything. It was possible the Indian would just ride away and think no more about the white man he had seen on the other side of the river. Or he might fetch a war party and be waiting somewhere downstream. Fargo couldn't afford to worry about that. He had to push on.

Later in the afternoon, he heard the roaring of a waterfall somewhere in front of him. He soon came to the first of the falls that led down to the plains. It was a spectacular sight. The bluffs along the banks lowered, the river spread out into a mighty stream hundreds of yards wide, and countless tons of water cascaded over a rocky brink to plunge about thirty feet into a spray-shrouded maelstrom.

Fargo stopped as he caught sight of a place where a fire had been built. He dismounted and checked the ashes, estimating that they were less than a day old. When he looked around, he found two different sets of footprints and recognized them as belonging to Mallory and Victoria.

He sighed in relief. Victoria was still alive—or at least she had been earlier today. Mallory must have paused here and prepared a meal before starting the descent to the plains.

Fargo let the Ovaro blow, then swung up into the saddle and pressed on. He made his way down a game trail next to the falls, glad that he had the sure-footed stallion under him.

There were four more falls, some of them fairly short, before the river reached the plains. The final cataract was the tallest of the five, and the spray that rose from it hung over the river like a perpetual fog. Fargo reached the bottom late in the day.

He was out of the mountains now. It was only about sixty miles to Fort Benton. Mallory had kept Victoria alive so far, but he couldn't afford to for much longer. Despite the cold and Fargo's own exhaustion, he kept riding.

To his right, the river widened out even more. Eventually it would become shallow and muddy. People said of the Platte River that the water was too thick to drink and too thin to plow, but the Missouri was almost as bad in places.

The wind picked up again. Fargo thought there might be another bout of snow before the night was over.

Suddenly, a whoop sounded behind him. He looked

back and saw several riders galloping after him. Muzzle flashes split the overcast gloom as they opened fire.

Fargo leaned forward over the Ovaro's neck and urged the stallion into a run. He didn't expect the Indians who were chasing him to be able to hit him with rifle shots fired from horseback, but he might as well give them as small a target as possible.

He was almost certain that one of his pursuers was the Indian he had seen on the far side of the river earlier that day. As Fargo had thought might happen, the man had gotten some of his fellow warriors to join him, and had hurried downstream to come after the white man who had invaded their hunting grounds. There were only a handful of them. They probably just wanted a little sport before the long, boring winter set in, and Fargo was going to provide it for them.

Chances were, their ponies were fresher than the stallion was, but Fargo knew what incredible stamina the Ovaro possessed. The horse would give his absolute all if Fargo asked for it.

And that might be what was needed for him to get away. He urged the horse on, calling on the stallion's reserves of strength.

Fargo looked back toward the mountains again. The Blackfeet had closed the gap a little. Now they were close enough that Fargo could see there were four of them. If it came to a fight, four-to-one odds weren't good, but he had faced worse in his life and survived.

The problem out here on the prairie was that there was no cover, no place to fort up and make a stand. Just miles and miles of mostly flat grassland.

So when Fargo saw the wagon, he thought at first that he was imagining things. Then, as his eyes fastened on it, he realized it was no illusion. The burned-out hulk of an abandoned wagon sat beside the river, black against the light dusting of snow on the ground.

Fargo didn't pause to wonder what the wagon was doing there. The story was plain enough. Some pilgrim had started this way from Fort Benton and had made it this far before Indians had wiped him out. The man's bones had probably been scattered across the prairie by wolves and other scavengers.

But right now, what was left of that luckless soul's wagon might prove to be Fargo's salvation. He headed straight for it, the Ovaro stretching his legs in a pounding gallop.

Fargo checked over his shoulder again. The pursuers were even closer now. They must have seen the wagon, too, and wanted to catch Fargo before he could reach it.

Fargo said to the Ovaro, "Come on, boy," the urgency in his voice spurring on the big horse. The stallion stretched out even more, sweeping over the ground at dizzying speed. If he stepped in a prairie-dog hole or something like that, the resulting fall would be catastrophic—likely fatal for both horse and rider.

But that didn't happen, as the sure-footed, keen-eyed stallion neatly avoided any obstacles and a few moments later pounded up to the ruined wagon.

With the Henry rifle clutched in his hands, Fargo was out of the saddle before the Ovaro came to a complete stop. He swung around behind the wagon and lifted the rifle to his shoulder. A bullet from one of the Indians' rifles ricocheted with a loud whine off an iron brace on the vehicle. They were only about fifty yards away.

Fargo fired rapidly, tolling off five shots as fast as he could work the lever and press the trigger. One of the Indians went flying off his pony. The other three gave up their direct charge and split apart, two veering to Fargo's left while the other went to the right.

Fargo tracked that one with the barrel of the Henry

and squeezed off a shot, but the Indian ducked down along the neck of his mount and the slug missed him.

As the warriors began to circle the wagon, Fargo grabbed the Ovaro's reins and dragged the horse to the ground. Having been through fights like this before, the stallion knew to lay flat, as much out of the way of bullets as possible. Then Fargo bellied down under the wagon. Lead thudded into the vehicle's frame above him.

With some men who are exceptionally good at killing, their nature is to hate taking life of any kind. Skye Fargo was that sort of man. Though it pained him to do so, he drew a bead on one of the Indian ponies and shot it. The pony's front legs folded up, and it crumpled to the ground, throwing its rider over its head. The Indian slammed into the ground and rolled over a couple of times, then lay there apparently stunned.

Seeing that Fargo intended to shoot their ponies and set them afoot, the other two Indians hurriedly tried to draw off out of range. Fargo fired two quick shots and saw one of the Indians fall. He thought the other one sagged forward, but the warrior managed to stay mounted. Fargo was pretty sure he had hit the man, though.

So three were down and one was wounded and running away. The wounded man might go back to his tribe and gather more warriors to come after Fargo, but that would take time. Fargo intended to be at Fort Benton before that threat could materialize.

There was still the Indian who had been thrown from his pony, plus the two Fargo had shot. He reloaded the Henry, replacing the cartridges he had used, and then cautiously left the cover of the wagon after a low-voiced command to the Ovaro to stay put.

The light was fading. Fargo approached the closest of the fallen Indians, who happened to be the one he had shot first. The man was dead, his throat torn away by Fargo's bullet. A look at the man's buckskins and paint and feathers confirmed that he was a Blackfoot.

He was also young, probably not more than twenty. Fargo's jaw tightened when he saw that. Four young braves, out hunting a white man. And Fargo made no mistake about it: They had been warriors despite their youth, and if they had caught him, he would have been just as dead as if they had been grizzled veterans of the plains wars. Still, he hated that he had been forced to snuff out such young lives.

The second Blackfoot was also dead, but the one who had been thrown from his horse was alive and starting to stir. Fargo hooked a boot toe under his shoulder and rolled him over onto his back, none too gently. He pointed the muzzle of the Henry at the young man's face.

"Your life is mine to do with as I will," Fargo told him in the Blackfoot tongue. "What would you have me do with it? Should I kill you or let you return to your people?"

Fargo saw the emotions warring on the young man's face. His sense of honor wanted Fargo to pull the trigger and kill him. That way he would not have to go back to his people in disgrace. But the young, beating heart did not want to die. It wanted the warrior to live to see the seasons change, to watch a family grow, and finally to grow old—then the heart would stop beating in the fullness of days.

"Your life is mine to do with as I will," Fargo said again. "So I give it to you." He stepped back. "Fight me if you wish, and there will be no bad blood between us. We will do battle as honored enemies. Or there is the pony of one of your brothers, that will carry you back to your people. The choice is yours."

The young man scrambled to his feet. His hand started toward the knife at his belt. He stopped before he touched it and stared at Fargo for a long moment, and then he turned and ran after one of the loose ponies. Fargo let him go, but he stood ready with the Henry until the young warrior had caught the pony and ridden away, vanishing toward the mountains.

Then Fargo heaved a sign and went back to the charred wagon to get the Ovaro.

He had ridden perhaps another mile when he saw the tiny winking eye of a campfire up ahead.

8

Fargo reined the Ovaro to a stop and sat in the saddle for a long moment, looking at the distant fire. He figured it was at least a mile off. Out here on the prairie, such things were visible from a long way away.

Mallory was an idiot. Fargo had already suspected as much from seeing the remains of the other fires left behind by the man. There were several hostile tribes in this part of the country besides the Crow and the Blackfoot, including the Sioux and the Cheyenne. Building a fire in the open was just asking to be noticed, especially here on the plains. Mallory and Victoria were lucky that they still had their hair.

Fargo suspected Mallory hadn't been out on the frontier that long. The man had probably heard about the gold seekers headed to Idaho and had come out to prey on them, putting together the gang after he'd got here. He was a vicious killer—no doubt about that—but something of a greenhorn in the ways of the West.

Fargo clucked to the Ovaro and sent the horse forward at a walk. Night had fallen, and already the air was quite cold.

When he was about a quarter of a mile away from the fire, Fargo dismounted and drew the Henry from its sheath. He started forward on foot. The stallion would stay where he was until Fargo called him.

No one was moving around the fire. As Fargo got closer he made out the two shapes sitting side by side near the flames. He went to his knees and then his belly, crawling forward over the cold ground.

He went ahead slowly and silently, not wanting to give Mallory any warning. Mallory's horse was picketed off to one side, cropping the short, mostly dead grass. The wind was in Fargo's face, so he didn't think the horse would scent either him or the Ovaro.

He heard voices as Mallory and Victoria talked, though he couldn't make out the words just yet. As he crawled closer, the wind carried a snatch of conversation to him.

". . . can go to hell, Mallory," Victoria was saying.

A faint grin tugged at Fargo's mouth. Victoria was nothing if not plain-spoken.

"Shut up, bitch," Mallory growled. "I been listenin' to you complain for three days now, and I'm gettin' tired of it. You'll be singin' a different tune here pretty soon, when I get through with you."

"You've been threatening to rape me for three days, too," Victoria shot back at him. "You haven't done it yet, so why should I be afraid now?"

Fargo was surprised but relieved to hear that Mallory hadn't attacked her yet. He kept edging closer and closer to the fire.

If Mallory and Victoria had been sitting on opposite sides of the flames, he would have risked standing up and taking a shot at Mallory. But they were too close together for that. The chance of hitting Victoria would be too great.

"I know now Fargo ain't after us," Mallory said in response to her question. "Now I can take my time and have some fun with you. It'll take us a couple more nights to get to Fort Benton, and I'm gonna ride you hard and put you up wet, lady."

Victoria gave a contemptuous snort.

Mallory cursed and swung his arm. His hand cracked across her face in a brutal slap. Fargo restrained his own anger. He hoped Victoria wouldn't continue to provoke the outlaw.

It was a futile hope. As Mallory drew back his hand to strike again, she lunged at him, trying to claw his face. He grabbed her wrists and shoved her back down on the ground. She kicked at him, but he flung himself on top of her, attempting to pin her down with his weight.

Fargo had waited as long as he could. His muscles tensed as he readied himself to spring up and rush into the camp.

He froze at the last instant as another figure stepped into the circle of light cast by the fire. The newcomer was a tall, buckskinned man who struck with blinding speed, smashing the butt of a rifle into the back of Mallory's head with one vicious stroke. Mallory sagged against Victoria, knocked cold by the blow.

Victoria looked up past the unconscious man's shoulder and screamed as the Indian reached for her. In the firelight, Fargo saw that the man's left hand was deformed, either by accident or birth. It was curved more like the talon of an animal than a human hand.

Fargo knew he was looking at the Crow war chief, Broken Hand.

The Indian kicked Mallory aside and grabbed Victoria's coat. He jerked her to her feet and pulled her against him. Fargo had the Henry at his shoulder, ready to fire, but he didn't dare press the trigger as long as Victoria was between him and Broken Hand. He waited for his chance.

It didn't come. The hand holding the rifle struck Victoria a short, wicked blow, stunning her. Broken

Hand bent his knees a little, got his left arm around her, and lifted her, throwing her over his shoulder.

Fargo was about to try a shot at Broken Hand's legs, hoping to cripple him, when the war chief called into the darkness, "Fargo! I know you are out there! You hear me, Fargo?"

With his pulse hammering madly, Fargo made no response, but he waited to hear what Broken Hand had to say.

"I have your woman now, Fargo," Broken Hand went on. "Come after me if you dare. She dies tomorrow when the sun is in the middle of the sky, at the place of the buffalo bones. Come watch me kill her, and then I will kill you, Fargo!"

Sensing that his time had run out, Fargo came up on his knees and fired. But Broken Hand was already darting back into the shadows, moving fast in the night, and a laugh told Fargo that his shot had missed. A moment later, he heard the pounding of hoofbeats.

Fargo surged to his feet and ran forward, cursing. He stopped to let out a high-pitched whistle. A moment later, the Ovaro raced up, reaching the camp about the same time as Fargo.

Fargo's brain worked quickly. Broken Hand had set the rendezvous, and he would keep Victoria alive until then . . . unless Fargo crossed him. If he went after the war chief now, Broken Hand might go ahead and kill Victoria right away. Fargo hated to think of how terrified she must be as Broken Hand's captive, but he knew the best chance of keeping her alive for the time being was to not pursue the Indian.

Mallory lay facedown. He moaned and stirred, trying awkwardly to push himself to his hands and knees. Normally, Fargo wouldn't kick a man while he was down, but he made an exception in Mallory's case. His boot toe dug into Mallory's side and knocked the outlaw sprawling on his back.

"You son of a bitch," Fargo grated as he bent over to pluck Mallory's gun from its holster. He pulled a Bowie knife from its sheath at the man's waist. Then he backed off a step and kept the barrel of the rifle pointed at Mallory's face.

Mallory blinked in confusion for a second before his eyes widened in fear and understanding. The Henry's muzzle must have looked as big around as a cannon—and as menacing—from that position.

"Don't . . . don't kill me, Fargo!" he croaked.

Fargo thought about how the young Blackfoot warrior had reacted in a very similar situation earlier. The youngster had been prepared to die rather than beg for his life. Mallory had no such sense of honor.

"Give me one good reason not to blow your damned head off," Fargo growled.

"I . . . I didn't hurt that woman. I could have, but I didn't do it. I swear I didn't!"

"You ran off with her in the first place," Fargo pointed out. "You've terrified her for days now. You would have raped her and killed her before you got to Fort Benton. Now Broken Hand has carried her off. You deserve a bullet, Mallory."

A cunning light came into the outlaw's eyes. Fargo saw it and wasn't surprised what by came out of Mallory's mouth next.

"Broken Hand's the one who clouted me and took Mrs. Landon? I'll help you get her back from that Injun, Fargo. You got my word on that. Let me live, and I'll back your play." Mallory licked his lips. "We fought side by side before. We can do it again."

Fargo thought about not only the hell through which Mallory had put Victoria, but also about the way the man had shot Two Bears in cold blood on two separate occasions.

But as much as Fargo disliked the idea, it was just

possible Mallory might be able to help him rescue Victoria from Broken Hand.

Fargo knew Mallory was a treacherous bastard and didn't trust him for a second. However, Broken Hand might not expect the two of them to team up again. Clearly, Broken Hand had been spying on Fargo ever since the Trailsman had left Poudre River Pete's trading post, and the war chief was cunning enough to figure out that Mallory had kidnapped Victoria. That was why he had gone after her; to use her as bait and to cause Fargo even more misery by threatening her life.

Fargo's finger was taut on the trigger of the Henry. He forced himself to ease off.

"All right," he said. "I won't kill you, and you can ride with me. You're not getting your gun back, though."

"I ain't goin' to be any good to you without a gun," Mallory complained.

"We'll worry about that later. Right now, get up off the ground and keep your mouth shut."

Fargo put Mallory's gun and knife in his saddlebags. Mallory didn't have a rifle.

"You got any coffee?" Mallory asked peevishly. "I ain't had any coffee since I don't know when."

"It was three days ago at the trading post," Fargo pointed out.

"Yeah, but I couldn't enjoy that, not with those savages a-yelpin' and a-hollerin' for our scalps."

Fargo had coffee. He got the small pot from his gear and dumped in water and coffee and put it on to boil. He still didn't like the idea of having a fire, but he decided he was willing to risk it so that he could keep a better eye on Mallory by its light.

He knew one thing: He wasn't going to close his eyes as long as Mallory was around.

When the coffee was ready, Mallory poured a cup for himself and sat huddled over it. After a few sips of the steaming brew, he asked, "You got any idea how we'll go about gettin' Mrs. Landon away from the Injun?"

Fargo poured some coffee, too, and warmed his fingers on the cup as he sat on the other side of the fire from Mallory. "Broken Hand told us where to find them."

"He did?" Mallory shook his head. "Reckon I must've been too addle-pated from gettin' hit in the head. I didn't hear anything like that."

"The place of the buffalo bones," Fargo said quietly.

"Where's that? I never heard of it," Mallory said, confirming Fargo's guess that the outlaw hadn't been in these parts for very long.

"It's between here and Fort Benton," Fargo explained. "I've been there before. There's a steep bluff, and the Sioux sometimes stampede a buffalo herd over it. The fall kills a lot of the buffalo and saves the Indians the trouble of killing them one at a time. They don't like to do it that way, though. Not as much honor in it."

Mallory grunted. "Killin' is killin'. Honor ain't got a damn thing to do with it."

Fargo would have expected that sort of attitude from the man who had bushwhacked Two Bears. He didn't say anything, just sipped the coffee, grateful for its heat as an icy wind scoured the plains.

The silence seemed to bother Mallory. "So there's lots of buffalo bones there, huh?" he said after a few minutes.

"That's right. Sometimes so many buffalo are killed that the Indians can't pack off all the meat before it rots, so they just take the hides and leave the rest of the carcasses there. It's wasteful, and normally they don't waste anything when they kill a buffalo. They use every bit of it. That's another reason they don't like to stampede the herds."

"Why do they do it, then?"

"If it's been a bad hunting season and they come across a large herd, they need to take as much advantage of it as they can. A warrior's honor is a mighty important thing, but so is putting food in the bellies of his wife and children, and robes on their backs."

"You almost sound like you admire them filthy savages."

Fargo just looked at Mallory and smiled. He much preferred the company of some of the Indians he had known to that of this outlaw. Mallory must have understood the meaning of Fargo's look, because he frowned darkly and muttered to himself for a second as he stared down into his coffee cup.

After a few moments, Mallory said, "You claim this buffalo bones place is where the Sioux stampede the critters. Broken Hand is a Crow, ain't he? How does he know about it?"

"The Crows get around, too—and not only that, they hear stories. I don't know if Broken Hand has ever been there before, but he knows it's close to the river. He can find it." Fargo paused before adding, "And we'll find him."

"And when we do, we kill him and take the woman back," Mallory said.

Fargo nodded. He noticed that Mallory didn't say anything about what would happen after that.

That was because then their temporary alliance would be over, and Mallory would do his best to kill Fargo, too. Fargo knew as much, but he would deal with that problem when it came up. Right now he was just worried about getting Victoria safely away from Broken Hand.

The night was going to be a long one. He poured himself another cup of coffee.

* * *

Later, it began to snow again. Fargo didn't mind the cold too much, because it helped him stay awake, but he didn't like the idea of snow. However, when he thought about it, he didn't suppose it would make much difference. It wasn't like he had to follow a trail anymore. He knew where Broken Hand had taken Victoria, and as long as he could follow the river, Fargo was confident he could find the place.

The snow made it more difficult to keep the fire going, though. Fargo rigged a blanket on some sticks to give the flames some protection from the wind, and he kept feeding buffalo chips into the fire all night. Mallory wrapped up in a blanket and lay down to sleep, prompting a disgusted look from Fargo, who couldn't afford to do that.

He knew that if he did, Mallory would murder him without hesitation.

The night was a miserable one, but like all nights, good or bad, it finally passed. The wind died down along toward dawn, but the snow continued falling. Heavy flakes drifted thickly to the ground now that they weren't being blown around by the wind.

Holding the Henry ready in his hands, Fargo roused Mallory by putting a booted foot on his shoulder and shoving. "Wake up," Fargo said. "It's time we were riding."

Mallory rolled over and groaned, then pushed himself into a sitting position, scattering the snow that had collected on his blanket during the night. He looked around. "Damn, it's still comin' down, ain't it?"

"That's right, and the sooner we start moving around, the less chance of us freezing to death," Fargo pointed out.

Mallory stumbled to his feet. "Ain't we gonna eat breakfast first?"

"We can eat in the saddle." Fargo's flat, hard tone left no room for argument.

He cast a worried look at the sky as he saddled the Ovaro. Broken Hand had said that Victoria would die at midday. With it snowing so hard, how in blazes was anybody going to know when that was? Fargo asked himself.

All he and Mallory could do was ride on and hope they got to the rendezvous in time. After everything Victoria had gone through, to have her murdered now by Broken Hand, when they were only two days' ride from Fort Benton . . .

He wouldn't let that happen, Fargo vowed. He would do everything in his power to prevent it.

Mallory had some jerky of his own in his saddlebags. He gnawed on it as he and Fargo plodded along through the falling snow. Fargo had the same sort of meager breakfast, supplemented by a stale biscuit.

The ground was completely white now, covered by a couple inches of snow instead of the dusting that had been there the day before. In another month, the snow would be several feet deep. The river would have a solid sheet of ice over it that would remain in place until the spring thaw. Winter was a harsh, desolate season in this lonely land, but for those hardy enough to endure it, there were rewards aplenty in the spring and summer.

Fargo hoped that he and Victoria would both live to see next spring. If they could survive and make it to Fort Benton, they could spend the winter there in relative comfort.

Mallory shivered and trembled, even in his heavy coat. "Lord, I wish I'd never come out here!" he said fervently.

Fargo had no real desire to make conversation with the outlaw, yet he heard himself saying, "Where are you from?"

"St. Louis. Grew up on the riverfront there. It was a mighty rough life, but now I wish I'd stayed."

"Why didn't you?"

"Oh, last spring I heard about those ol' boys who found gold out in Idaho Territory. Thought I'd come out and try my hand at prospectin'. I never got there, though. I fell in with that bunch I was with, and it didn't take me long to find out that I was tougher than any of 'em." There was pride in Mallory's voice as he spoke. "That's how I come to be runnin' the gang."

"So you don't deny that you and your men were outlaws?"

"Oh, hell, no. A lot of those fellas on their way to the goldfields had mighty nice prospectin' outfits, and some of them even had a stake of cash. We'd hold them up, take what they had, keep the cash, and sell the rest of the gear to some other bunch of pilgrims who came along later. Then we'd turn around and steal the stuff from them, too. Made a pretty good haul for a few months before the weather started gettin' worse and the prospectin' parties stopped comin' along." Mallory spat into the snow. "That's why we were headin' for Fort Benton when we had the bad luck to run into you, Fargo. How were we to know you were draggin' so much trouble along behind you?"

Even now, Mallory managed to make himself sound like the injured party, Fargo thought. A man like that would always lay the blame for his problems on someone else, he supposed.

They stayed close to the clay banks that rose above the river. Even Fargo's keen eyes couldn't see more than about fifty yards through the thickly falling flakes.

"Lord, can't we rest for a spell?" Mallory asked. "We been ridin' for hours."

"It just seems like it's been hours," Fargo said.

"We'll push on a while longer before we take a break."

"When are you gonna give me my gun back?"

"When you need it."

"What if that redskin kills you? Then he'll come after me, and I'll be unarmed. Won't even be able to defend myself."

Fargo didn't say anything. He didn't feel like arguing with Mallory. After a few moments with no response, the outlaw began muttering resentfully again. Fargo ignored him.

Out here on the prairie, there weren't many landmarks. The heavy snow prevented Fargo from seeing the ones that did exist. He tried to estimate how far he and Mallory had come since leaving the camp that morning. He thought the place of the buffalo bones was about ten miles north of that spot, and it seemed that he and Mallory had been riding long enough to cover that much distance, even at the slow pace they had been forced into by the weather.

Suddenly, Fargo reined in sharply and thrust out a hand, motioning for Mallory to do likewise. He heard something. A thin sound that cut through the cold, heavy air.

A woman's scream.

"Son of a bitch!" Mallory exclaimed. "That sounds like Mrs. Landon!"

One scream sounded pretty much like another, but chances were, Victoria was the only woman out here in this snowy wilderness today. The sound came from the left. Fargo wheeled the Ovaro around and heeled the big stallion into a run.

"Fargo!" Mallory shouted after him. "Fargo, give me a gun!"

Fargo slowed a little and reached inside his coat as Mallory's horse pounded up alongside him. He pulled out Mallory's six-gun and passed it over to the outlaw.

He didn't trust Mallory, but he couldn't leave the man defenseless while a revenge-crazed Crow war chief was running around loose somewhere close by.

The Ovaro surged ahead again, answering Fargo's demand for more speed. Snow flew up from his hooves as he swept over the ground. The bluff where the Sioux stampeded the buffalo was about five hundred yards away from the river, Fargo recalled. He didn't slow down until he judged that the stallion had covered almost that much distance.

His guess was right. He hauled back on the reins, bringing the big black-and-white horse to a stop as the ground fell away steeply in front of them.

Fargo swung down from the saddle, taking the Henry with him. Leaving the Ovaro, he ran along the bluff. There was a trail down to the bottom, he recalled from the last time he had ridden by this place.

Victoria screamed again.

Fargo muttered a curse. "Broken Hand!" he bellowed into the snow. "Broken Hand, I'm here!"

Maybe that would make the Crow hold off on whatever he was doing to Victoria. Broken Hand had said that he wanted Fargo to watch her die. That goal was almost within his reach.

Fargo threw a glance over his shoulder. He had lost track of Mallory and didn't know if the outlaw had followed him or not. He was well aware that he had two enemies to deal with, not just one. Mallory couldn't be relied on to help him rescue Victoria from Broken Hand. Now that he was armed again, the outlaw might just ride on, abandoning Fargo and Victoria to their fates, whatever they turned out to be.

Or he might lie in wait somewhere nearby in hopes of killing either Fargo or Broken Hand—whichever one survived the next few minutes—and then recapturing Victoria. Either way, Fargo knew that he was on his own again.

He found the trail and started down it, being careful not to slip on the snow. The bluff was a good fifty feet high. If he fell that far, he could break a leg or his back, and then Broken Hand could take his time killing him. The torture that would involve would be long and agonizing. . . .

"Fargo! You hear me, Fargo?" It was Broken Hand's voice.

"I'm here!" Fargo shouted back. "Victoria, can you hear me?"

Broken Hand's laugh floated out of the whiteness. "Your woman still lives, Fargo. She has done her chore. Her screams have brought you to me. Come, Fargo. Come to your death."

Fargo was almost to the bottom of the bluff. Since he didn't know where Victoria was, he couldn't try shooting at the sound of Broken Hand's voice. She might be in the way. He would have to confront the war chief, meet Broken Hand face-to-face. That was the only way he could be sure that Victoria was safe.

"If you want a fight, I'll give you a fight!" he shouted. "Guns, knives, bare hands! Whatever you want, Broken Hand!"

He was at the bottom of the trail. He started forward, and in the misty light he saw the piles of bones stacked haphazardly around him. White on white, the remains of thousands of buffalo that had fallen to their deaths here in this place. The snow swirled and drifted and grew deeper, but it would have a hard time covering all the bones that surrounded Skye Fargo.

Sometimes a small bone rolled under his foot as he stalked forward. He kept his balance, kept moving. His heart thudded heavily, and every muscle in his body was tense. His nerves were as taut as they could be.

"Broken Hand!" he shouted again. "Where are you?"

"Here, Fargo!"

The clouds of softly falling snow parted a little, and Fargo saw Victoria. She stood with her arms outstretched, each wrist lashed to one of the grisly piles that flanked her, like a human sacrifice on an altar of bones. Her hair hung loose. She had a strip of cloth tied around her head, holding a gag in her mouth. Fargo saw a thin line of red on her cheek and knew that Broken Hand must have slashed her with his knife to make her scream. Other than that, however, she seemed to be unharmed.

She might not stay that way for long. Broken Hand stood beside her, rifle in his good hand. He pointed the barrel at her head as he beckoned to Fargo with his deformed hand.

"Come closer, Fargo," Broken Hand said.

"Why don't you let her go?" Fargo asked, even as he moved closer. "This is between you and me, Broken Hand. I'm the one you want to kill."

"You are the one I want to *suffer,*" Broken Hand said, his face twisting with hatred. "The warriors who followed me were ashamed that we failed to kill you. They were ashamed that we were forced to run from the Blackfeet. All but three said that they would follow me no more."

"The three who came with you after me," Fargo guessed.

"Yes, and you killed them. Now the only way I can regain my honor and return to my people as their war chief is to kill you, Fargo, and take your head back with me."

"That won't change a thing," Fargo said. "You'll never regain what you lost in their eyes, Broken Hand."

"You lie! They will see that I killed the famous Skye Fargo! I, Broken Hand!"

Victoria lifted her head a little, so that Fargo could see her eyes. They were wide with horror and pain.

"If my death is what you really want, again I say for you to face me man to man. Let the woman go, so that she can travel on to Fort Benton and tell everyone there what a mighty war chief Broken Hand is."

Broken Hand sneered. "You think me a fool." He brought the barrel of the rifle closer to Victoria's head. "No, the woman dies first, before your eyes."

Fargo snapped the Henry to his shoulder. "You pull the trigger and you'll be dead a second later!" he warned. "I won't miss!"

Broken Hand looked around at him. "What of *your* honor, Fargo?"

"I don't give a damn about it right now," Fargo replied honestly. "You hurt her again and your brains will be on the snow."

For a long moment, the tense tableau held. Then, with a roar of rage, Broken Hand jerked the barrel of his rifle toward Fargo and pulled the trigger.

Fargo was already diving forward as Broken Hand's rifle cracked. He fired as he hit the ground and saw Broken Hand jerk backward as the slug struck him. But the war chief stayed on his feet and ducked under Victoria's right arm, darting behind her so that Fargo couldn't fire again. Fargo heard the slap of Broken Hand's moccasins against the snow-covered ground as the Indian ran around the piles of bones.

Fargo rolled to the side, knowing that Broken Hand would try to stalk him through this eerie graveyard. He wanted to rush over to Victoria and cut her loose, but if he did he would draw Broken Hand's fire toward her. Quickly, Fargo circled in the same direction the war chief had gone.

A shot blasted out, and the bullet whipped past

Fargo's head to pulverize a bone in the pile behind him. Fargo caught a glimpse of the muzzle flash and threw a shot back at it.

He was sure that Broken Hand was wounded, but he didn't know how badly. He didn't know where Mallory was, either. It was beginning to look as if the outlaw had deserted him. That was all right, Fargo supposed. He would have liked to bring Mallory to justice, but he would trade that satisfaction for Victoria's life.

Something rattled to his left. He started to turn in that direction, then stopped short as he realized the noise had been a trick.

The realization came too late. With a hoarse shout, Broken Hand charged out of the snow and crashed into Fargo. Both men fell. The Henry slipped out of Fargo's hands and slithered away on the snowy ground.

Fargo jerked his head to the side as Broken Hand slashed at him with a knife. Broken Hand had thrown away his gun, probably because he really did want to kill Fargo with his own hands. Fargo grabbed Broken Hand's wrist and rolled over, hauling the Indian with him. The fingers of Fargo's other hand fell on something hard and smooth. He snatched it up and lashed out with it.

The makeshift club was a buffalo bone. It slammed into Broken Hand's shoulder. The war chief cried out in pain. Fargo struck again, aiming at Broken Hand's elbow this time. When the blow landed, Broken Hand's fingers opened reflexively and he dropped the knife.

He clawed at Fargo's face with his other hand. Fargo felt the nails dig into his skin and draw blood as they slid down to Fargo's neck. But the war chief couldn't close those malformed fingers to choke him. Fargo used the bone to bat the hand aside. He drew the club back for another blow, this one aimed at Broken Hand's head.

Before it could fall, Broken Hand managed to raise his leg and hook his ankle at the side of Fargo's neck. With a cry of effort, he flung the Trailsman aside. Fargo rolled across the ground. Broken Hand sprang up and came after him.

Fargo came to a stop on his back. He saw that Broken Hand had grabbed the knife from the ground and was about to drive it down into Fargo's chest. The Trailsman snapped his leg up in a kick that drove deep into Broken Hand's belly. The Indian's momentum carried him forward, and Fargo helped him along by reaching up and hauling hard on Broken Hand's buckskin shirt as he pivoted his leg up and over.

With a startled yell, Broken Hand went over Fargo and sailed through the air to crash heavily into the base of a bone pile.

Fargo rolled over and pushed himself to his feet. He heard a rattling and crunching and saw that the pile of bones Broken Hand had slammed into was starting to shift. The war chief was stunned, but he regained his senses in time to look up and scream as tons of bones rolled down on top of him, crushing the life from him.

Fargo was a little stunned himself, and somewhat horrified by the grotesque end to Broken Hand's threat. He shook his head and started to look around for his hat and his rifle. He found them and hurried back through the jungle of bones to the place where Victoria had been tied. He was anxious to cut her free and get her out of this place.

But when Fargo got there, she was gone.

9

Fargo threw his head back and roared, "Mallory!"

The fat snowflakes continued to fall around him, mocking in their soft silence.

Fargo took a deep breath and brought the rage he felt under control. He couldn't do Victoria any good if he was too angry to think straight. He looked around, trying to see what he could learn by the signs that had been left behind.

He saw a welter of footprints in the snow: his own, the moccasin tracks left by the late and unlamented Broken Hand, and Victoria's. And another set of boot prints that had to belong to Smoky Jack Mallory.

Fargo saw something else on the snow that set his blood to boiling again. Little droplets of crimson that had spattered the white snow. The blood must have come from the knife slash on Victoria's cheek, Fargo thought.

The rawhide thongs that had bound her to the bone piles had been cut. Mallory must have had a knife hidden somewhere on him, because Fargo had taken his Bowie and never returned it.

The tracks led back toward the bluff. Fargo picked up his rifle and followed them.

Though the snow was still falling heavily, it wasn't coming down fast enough to fill up the footprints Mallory and Victoria had left behind. The prints led to the trail that went up the bluff. Fargo climbed it quickly, knowing there was nowhere else Mallory could go with his prisoner.

When he reached the top of the bluff, he whistled for the Ovaro. The stallion ran up, tossing his head eagerly. Fargo wondered briefly if Mallory had tried to catch the stallion. If he had, the attempt had been doomed to failure.

Fargo slid the Henry back in the saddle sheath and grabbed the reins. He swung up into the saddle and felt a little better right away. Mallory's horse couldn't outdistance the stallion. Fargo knew that.

Hc followed the tracks to the spot where Mallory had left his horse. Judging by the prints in the snow, Victoria hadn't struggled with her captor. She was probably in a state of shock, too stunned to fight back, Fargo thought. Most people would be in bad shape if they'd had to endure everything that Victoria had gone through in the past week or so. Her life had been threatened at every turn, and just as it seemed she might be safe again, she was snatched from one danger to the next.

Mallory had followed the river, taking Victoria with him. The Missouri was the only reliable landmark out here now. The rest of the Montana country had become a snow-covered, trackless wasteland.

Fargo could tell that Mallory was riding hard, pushing his mount for all it was worth. The outlaw had to be hoping that Fargo and Broken Hand had killed each other in their showdown, but he couldn't count on that. He had to be worried about one of them coming after him.

And Mallory was right to worry, Fargo thought grimly. The next time he saw the man, he intended to shoot him on sight. This deadly game between them had gone on long enough.

Fargo kept the Ovaro moving at a fast, steady clip—the sort of pace the stallion could keep up for a long time. After a while, the snow fall thinned out and then stopped completely. The sky overhead grew a bit lighter. The storm was moving on. If the clouds broke that night and the winds stayed light, the temperature would plummet well below freezing.

The Trailsman rode on through the afternoon. Late in the day, the sun came out and cast a dazzling red glare over the snowy landscape. Fargo's breath fogged thickly in front of his face.

This snowstorm was winter's way of saying hello. It wouldn't leave for another four or five months.

Fargo's head jerked up as he caught himself dozing in the saddle. How long had it been since he had slept? He didn't know, couldn't remember. Long enough so that exhaustion was a living thing inside him, coiling around his muscles like a snake. He dug out some jerky and chewed on it to give his strength a boost and help him stay awake.

It wouldn't do to ride into an ambush because he was too tired to stay alert.

Twilight began to settle over the countryside. Still, the tracks of Mallory's horse kept going, following the river. Fargo wondered if the outlaw intended to try to push on to Fort Benton without stopping. It was a long ride, and Mallory would probably kill his horse doing it, but he had already demonstrated that he didn't care about anybody or anything as long as he got what he wanted.

Fargo didn't stop when it got dark. He kept going, pausing only now and then for a few minutes at a time to let the Ovaro rest. That wasn't enough, and he knew it. He was wearing out the stallion. But he had to keep going, because Victoria was up there somewhere, being held prisoner by Mallory.

Ever since Mallory had ridden off from the trading

post with Victoria, Fargo had dreaded finding her body as he followed them. He had been convinced that sooner or later Mallory would kill her, rather than take her all the way to Fort Benton with him.

But now it seemed as if that was exactly what Mallory intended to do. Why had he changed his mind? Would he risk Victoria telling the authorities at the fort that he was a killer and a kidnapper?

Fargo couldn't answer those questions. All he could do was keep riding.

Stars came out overhead and shone brightly against the black backdrop of the heavens. There were millions of them—so many, in fact, that at first Fargo mistook the lights of Fort Benton for even more of them.

But then he realized that those glittering points of illumination were too low to the ground to be stars. Instead, they marked the last outpost of civilization in this part of the country.

He reined in, wearily scrubbed a hand over his face, and gave his head a little shake as he tried to throw off the exhaustion that gripped him. He took a deep breath, squared his shoulders, and felt stronger. He rode on.

The American Fur Company had built Fort Benton as a trading post, not a military fort. But it was as sturdy as any fort west of the Mississippi, with massively thick clay walls, heavy gates, and guard towers that rose at the northwest and southeast corners of the compound.

A good-sized town had grown up around the fort, with a number of wharves along the river where steamboats docked. In times of Indian trouble, all the citizens of the settlement could gather behind the walls and be relatively safe. The fur company had allowed a small garrison of Army troops to be stationed at Fort Benton as well, adding to the place's security.

Outside the fort, the settlement was much like scores of other frontier communities, with a main street lined by businesses and a few side streets where huts, cabins, and tents housed the settlers. The tepees of some friendly Indians could be found on the outskirts of town and along the river.

And like most frontier settlements, there were more saloons in Fort Benton than anything else. As the Ovaro plodded along the main street, Fargo kept a close eye on the horses tied at the hitch rails. He was looking for the animal Mallory had been riding.

The saloons were still doing a good business despite the late hour. As a man emerged from one of them, wrapped in a heavy fur coat that made him look a little like a bear as he shambled along the street, Fargo reined in and hailed him.

"Have you seen a man and a woman ride into town in the past half-hour or so?" the Trailsman asked.

The man in the fur coat peered up at Fargo and shook his head. "Nope, friend, I sure haven't. But I been in the saloon drinkin' for longer than that. Better ask somebody else."

Fargo nudged the Ovaro on and raised a hand in thanks. "Much obliged, anyway. Say, where's the best livery stable in town?"

Mallory might have headed straight for a stable rather than tying his horse in front of a saloon, Fargo thought.

The man in the fur coat pointed. "Three blocks further along, on the left, right up yonder by the fort. Fella they call Jersey Bill runs it."

Fargo nodded and rode on, still keeping an eye out for Mallory's horse. He hadn't come across it by the time he reached the stable, though.

Jersey Bill was a slender, wiry man with spectacles perched on his nose. He came out of the stable and looked at the Ovaro with frank admiration. Even in his tired state, the stallion was a magnificent specimen of horseflesh.

"Mighty nice horse, mister," he said to Fargo. "You looking to stable him for the winter, or just until the boat pulls out?"

"Boat?" Fargo repeated with a frown.

Jersey Bill pointed toward the Missouri River. "Yep, there's still one steamboat tied up at the docks. Last one out before all the river traffic shuts down until the spring. Folks who want to get back to St. Louis while they still can will be taking it."

Fargo glanced up and down the street, noticing the large number of horses and wagons. "Reckon that's why the settlement is so busy."

Jersey Bill nodded and said, "That's right. That riverboat will be a mite crowded. I'm sure they can find room for one more if you're of a mind to go, though."

"What about my horse?" Fargo asked as he swung down from the saddle.

"I'll buy him from you," the stableman said without hesitation. "I'm doing a pretty heavy business in horse-buying right now. But I'll have a good stock to sell come next spring when all the pilgrims heading west start to show up again."

Fargo patted the Ovaro's shoulder. "He's not for sale. He'll have to go with me if I go."

"You'll have to talk to the boat's captain about that. I'll be glad to find a stall for that stallion, though. Be an honor to have such a fine horse in my stable, even for one night."

Fargo handed over the reins and asked the question that had brought him here. "Have you seen a man and a woman come into town in the past half-hour? The man has red hair and a beard, and the woman has a cut on her face."

"Sure, they came in here," Jersey Bill answered without hesitation. He jerked a thumb over his shoulder.

"Their horse is back yonder in one of the stalls. Poor brute was so worn out I'm surprised it didn't just lay down and die as soon as they got off." The stableman frowned. "A man's got no right to push a horse so hard, especially one that's carrying double like that."

"The woman was all right?"

"Well, not really," Jersey Bill said. "Like you said, she's got that cut on her face, but that didn't look too bad. Mainly she just seemed beaten down, like she'd seen so much trouble that she didn't care anymore. I didn't like the looks of the fella who was with her, either. Had a mean way about him. She went with him without any fuss, though."

Fargo nodded. Jersey Bill didn't know how right he was about Smoky Jack Mallory being mean.

"Do you know where they went?"

"The man said they were looking for a place to stay until that riverboat pulls out tomorrow. I sent 'em back down the street to the Montana Belle Saloon. I think it's the only place in town that still has rooms to rent."

Fargo nodded and handed a gold piece to the stable keeper. "Much obliged. Take good care of my horse."

Jersey Bill grinned as he slipped the coin into his overalls. "I sure will, mister," he promised.

There was only a light breeze blowing as Fargo walked down the street toward the Montana Belle Saloon, but it was cold enough to cut right through the sheepskin coat he wore.

He wondered why Victoria was being so cooperative with Mallory? Perhaps the fighting spirit she had demonstrated at times had finally been destroyed. Maybe she had given up and decided it was easier just to go along with whatever the outlaw wanted.

There was no way of knowing what Mallory had told her. He might have said that he had seen Fargo killed by Broken Hand. In that case, Victoria probably would have preferred being "rescued" by Mallory to being left for the Crow war chief to kill.

The more Fargo thought about it, the more he was convinced that something along those lines had happened. Once Mallory convinced Victoria that she had to cooperate with him in order to save her own skin, he might have warned her not to say anything about what he had done in the past. If she believed that Fargo was dead, then she would think that it would be her word against her captor's.

Mallory probably thought he had her buffaloed, and that everything was going his way now.

He was in for one hell of a surprise, Fargo thought grimly.

The doors of the Montana Belle Saloon were tightly shut, but Fargo could hear the music and laughter coming from inside as he approached. The patrons of the saloon were having a final blowout before leaving on the last riverboat or settling down to wait out the long winter. Chances were, things wouldn't quiet down very much until morning.

Fargo went inside, stepping through the doors quickly and pulling them closed behind him so as not to let any more of the precious interior warmth escape than he had to.

As heat closed in around him, however, he decided that the place could use a little cooling off. Fires burned in a couple of cast-iron stoves, making the saloon uncomfortably stuffy. The thick haze of tobacco smoke didn't help matters, either.

Fargo looked around, his gaze darting along the bar and over the scattered tables, searching for Mallory. He didn't see the outlaw or Victoria Landon anywhere in the long, narrow room.

Unlike a lot of frontier buildings, the Montana Belle had a real second story, not just a false front. A balcony overhung a small dance floor in the rear of the saloon. Fargo saw several doors on the second floor and figured those were the rooms for rent that Jersey Bill had mentioned.

The bar was crowded, with men lined up two or three deep in places. Fargo made his way to it and shouldered a path through to the hardwood. A thick-bodied bartender, one of three men behind the bar, came up to him a few moments later and asked, "What can I do for you, mister? Whiskey?"

A drink sounded mighty good to Fargo, but considering how little food and sleep as he had gotten the past couple of days, he wasn't sure it would be a smart idea.

"Maybe later," he said. "Right now I'm looking for a man and a woman who came in here a little while ago. The man's got red hair and a beard, and the woman has a cut on her cheek."

The bartender shook his head. "Haven't seen 'em."

"Fella down at the livery stable said he sent them down here to rent a room for the night."

"I don't care, they ain't here."

Fargo's eyes narrowed. Mallory might have paid the bartender to lie about seeing him and Victoria, just on the off chance that Fargo would show up looking for them.

He slid a gold piece across the bar but kept his hand on it. "You sure about that?" he asked the bartender.

The man licked his lips, and Fargo could tell that he was tempted. That was another strong indication that Mallory and Victoria were here. But after a moment, the bartender gave a regretful shake of his head.

"Sorry, mister. I can't help you."

"Can't . . . or won't?"

The bartender's face hardened. "Look, if you don't want a drink, then move on. You're takin' up space a payin' customer could use."

Fargo slipped the gold piece back in his pocket and

turned away from the bar. He walked toward the door.

His mind was working rapidly. He was convinced Mallory and Victoria were upstairs in one of those rooms. Mallory had paid off the bartender and probably threatened him, too, just to make sure the man wouldn't reveal where they were if anybody asked.

Fargo stepped outside and pulled the door closed behind him, then moved to the left as if he intended to walk away from the place. But after a couple of steps he crouched and tried to look through the plate-glass window that had no doubt come up from St. Louis on one of the riverboats.

The glass was fogged up on the inside because of the heat in the saloon, which made it difficult to see through it. Fargo had only a distorted view of what was going on inside.

But he was fairly sure he spotted the bartender leaving his post and going upstairs to the second floor.

To warn Mallory that somebody was looking for him, maybe? Mallory could have slipped the man a little extra money to perform such a service.

Fargo straightened and hurried along the front of the saloon to the alley that ran alongside it, separating it from the next building. He ducked into the shadowy passageway.

There was probably a set of rear stairs leading up to the second floor, so that people could come and go unseen. That was a common arrangement in places where illicit activities occurred.

Sure enough, a narrow set of stairs climbed the back of the saloon to a tiny landing. Fargo started up the steps, catfooting along them in almost complete silence.

He unbuttoned his coat and swept it back as he approached the landing. His hand closed around the butt of the Colt.

When he reached the landing, he carefully tried the knob of the door there. It was locked.

Fargo put his ear against the door and listened closely. He thought he heard footsteps and maybe the sound of voices, but he couldn't be sure. The faint noises faded away, and all was quiet except for the racket coming from downstairs.

He took a chance, putting his shoulder against the door and shoving at the same time as he twisted the door knob. The barrier wasn't sturdy enough to withstand such pressure. The flimsy lock popped open.

Fargo drew his gun as he stepped into a short upstairs hallway that ended on the balcony he had seen from below. There was no lamp in the corridor, but enough light came from downstairs that he could see where he was going. Both walls were blank, with no doors.

He moved quietly to the end of the hall, stopping just before he reached the balcony. Leaning forward, he looked up and down the balcony. No one was there. The bartender must have already gone back downstairs.

A glance at the bar and the tables told Fargo that no one was paying any attention to what was happening on the second floor. The Montana Belle's customers were too concerned with their own drinking and carousing to care about anyone else's. Fargo didn't see the bartender he had talked to earlier, but the other two drink jugglers were still hard at work.

There were two doors to Fargo's left and three to his right. He had no idea which room Mallory had rented. He would have to listen at the thin doors and hope he heard a voice he recognized.

But he would be in plain sight as he did so, and all he could do was hope that no one would notice him and raise an alarm.

As he stepped out onto the balcony, it occurred to

him that he could have gone to the fort and told his story to the commander of the military garrison there. His sometimes bothersome reputation usually came in handy when he was trying to convince an Army officer that he was telling the truth. The commanding officer probably would have sent a detail of troops with him to search the saloon.

But that would have raised a commotion and maybe warned Mallory in time for him to hurt Victoria. Fargo didn't want to run that risk. It would be better to take Mallory by surprise.

Besides, he wanted to finish this himself. This showdown had been building ever since he and Mallory met.

He had just about reached the first door on his left when it suddenly opened. The bartender Fargo had spoken to earlier stepped out onto the balcony. His eyes widened in recognition and surprise as he saw the Trailsman standing there, gun drawn. His mouth opened to let out a yell.

Fargo struck first, balling his left hand into a fist and stepping forward to smash a blow to the man's jaw. The bartender didn't make a sound, but as he staggered backward he ran into the railing along the edge of the balcony. The railing shattered, sending the man plummeting off the balcony. He crashed onto one of the tables below, scattering cards and drinks. Men yelled and cursed in alarm and confusion.

So much for being quiet and taking Mallory by surprise, Fargo thought, as he swung into the doorway and brought his gun up.

A pistol blasted somewhere in front of him. The slug ripped splinters from the doorjamb beside his head. Fargo couldn't return the fire blindly because he hadn't located Victoria yet.

There she was, lying on the bed. She started up as she saw him, crying, "Skye!"

Mallory stepped behind her and looped an arm around her neck, jerking her up in front of him. Just as he had done at Poudre River Pete's trading post, he used her as a shield, jabbing his gun past her and triggering two more shots at Fargo.

Fargo threw himself forward as the bullets sizzled over his head. He didn't have a shot at Mallory's body—not as long as Victoria was in the way.

But Mallory's legs were spread wide for balance, so Fargo aimed at the right one and fired. Mallory howled in pain and staggered as the slug ripped through his calf.

Victoria drove an elbow back into Mallory's midsection. She tore free of his grip and flung herself over the bed, landing on the floor on the other side, well out of the line of fire.

The Colt in Fargo's hand roared twice, bucking against his palm. The bullets smashed into Mallory and drove him backward toward the room's single window. The outlaw managed to get one more shot off as he fell, but it thudded harmlessly into the floor. Mallory hit the window and the glass exploded outward around him. With a yell, he disappeared, toppling into the darkness.

Fargo scrambled to his feet and hurried over to kneel next to Victoria. She pushed herself up and clutched desperately at him.

"Skye!" she said in a half-sob. "Skye, is it really you? Mallory told me you were dead! He said he saw Broken Hand kill you and that the only chance I had to get away was to go with him. But then that bartender said somebody was downstairs looking for us, and when he described you, I . . . I didn't know what to believe!"

Fargo pulled her to him, cradling her against his chest with his strong arms. "I figured it must have happened something like that," he told her. "But I'm fine, and now you are, too. It's all over, Victoria."

The ominous clicking as gun hammers were eared back told Fargo that he might have spoken too soon.

He looked over his shoulder and saw several men crowding the doorway, pointing pistols and rifles at him. Among them were the other two bartenders, who probably weren't happy about what Fargo had done to their colleague. One of them said in loud, excited tones, "Hold it right there, mister! Drop that gun!"

"Take it easy," Fargo said, keeping his own voice calm. Moving slowly and carefully so as not to spook any of the nervous mob, he leaned over and placed his Colt on the bed. Then he straightened, helping Victoria to her feet as he did so.

"Now step away from that woman!" the man ordered.

"No!" Victoria said as she clutched at Fargo's coat. "You've got it all wrong. Skye rescued me."

The bartender lowered his pistol slightly and frowned. "What? I thought you was with that other fella. What happened to him, anyway?"

"He should be lying out there in the alley behind the saloon," Fargo said, adding bluntly, "I shot him."

"We figured as much," another man said as he brandished a Sharps. "What for? Fightin' over that gal?"

"Listen to me," Victoria said as she recovered some of her wits and her spirit. "This man is my friend. His name is Skye Fargo. That other man kidnapped me. In fact, he kidnapped me twice in the past week! His name is Mallory, and he's some sort of outlaw."

"I never heard of no owlhoot named Mallory," the owner of the Sharps said.

"No, but I've heard of Skye Fargo," a third man put in. "He's the one they call the Trailsman."

Striking while the iron was hot, Fargo said, "If you'll send word to the commanding officer at the fort, I reckon there's a good chance he'll vouch for me."

Most of the men gathered on the balcony had lowered their weapons by then, but they still looked confused. One of the bartenders said, "The gent who came in with the woman told us she was his wife, and he was taking her away from a fella she tried to run away with. Paid all three of us not to say anything if anybody came asking for them."

Fargo nodded. "I don't doubt it, but he was lying to you."

"He was," Victoria said. "I'm a widow. My late husband was the commanding officer down at Fort Newcomb. The garrison there was wiped out a week or so ago by a Crow war party. Mr. Fargo saved my life then, and ever since he's been trying to get me here safely to Fort Benton."

Her mention of the attack on Fort Newcomb started a hubbub. "Damn!" one man said. "We ain't heard nothin' about a massacre like that!"

"That's another reason we've been trying to get here," Fargo said, "so we could notify the Army of what's happened."

"Well, hell, mister. Sorry we jumped to the wrong conclusion." The bartender who had spoken earlier looked rather sheepish now. "You can understand how come we thought you were the troublemaker, though. Shoot, you knocked Howie clean off the balcony!"

"How is he?" Fargo asked. "I didn't really want to hurt him."

"He's out cold, but I reckon he'll be all right. Didn't seem to be any bones broken. That must've been one hell of a punch to send him flying like that. Howie's a pretty big fella."

"When he wakes up, I'll apologize," Fargo said. "Right now, can I pick up my gun again?"

The tense atmosphere had dissipated. "Sure, go ahead," the other bartender said.

Fargo holstered the Colt and turned to Victoria. "I want to go check on Mallory," he told her. "Will you be all right here?"

She nodded. "Go ahead. I'll feel better when I know he'll never bother us again."

Fargo left her in the room and went down the corridor to the rear staircase, most of the men trooping after him. He opened the door and looked out into the snowy alley, expecting to see Mallory's limp form sprawled darkly against the white covering on the ground.

Instead, Mallory was gone.

Fargo stiffened in surprise. "Anybody got a lantern?" he asked.

"I'll get a lamp from one of the rooms," one of the bartenders offered.

A minute later, Fargo started down the stairs with a lit lamp in one hand and the heavy revolver in the other. The glow from the lamp showed him where Mallory had fallen from the broken window, landed on the stairs, and then tumbled the rest of the way to the bottom. There were splotches of blood on most of the steps.

"He must've been hit good," one of the men looking over Fargo's shoulder said.

"Once in the leg and twice in the body."

Given the extent of Mallory's injuries, Fargo hadn't expected him to get up and walk away, but the tracks at the bottom of the stairs indicated that was exactly what he had done. Occasional splatters of blood marked his trail, too.

Fargo followed the footprints until they reached a

shed behind one of the other buildings. The door of the shed was open.

"Old Man Hastings keeps his mule in there," a member of the crowd said. "That fella Mallory must've stolen it."

Hoofprints led away from the shed, confirming that guess. The trail led northwest, away from Fort Benton and the Missouri River. There was nothing in that direction except a lot of open prairie and eventually the Rocky Mountains and the Canadian border.

Fargo thought about getting the Ovaro and going after Mallory, but after a moment he decided against it. In all likelihood, Mallory had passed out and fallen off the mule somewhere out there on the prairie, and by morning he would be dead. There was no way he could survive the frigid night, not as badly wounded as he was.

Fargo didn't want to leave Victoria again. She had been through enough.

"I'll talk to the commander at the fort," Fargo said. "He can alert his patrols to be on the lookout for Mallory's body. I reckon they'll bring it in, in a week or two."

"If the wolves leave anything of it," one of the men said.

Fargo nodded. It was entirely possible that Mallory's corpse would provide a meal for some of the gaunt gray predators that roamed the prairie.

He returned to the saloon and climbed the back stairs while the rest of the group went around through the front. Victoria was sitting on the bed when he came into the room where he had left her. She had her coat pulled tightly around her against the cold wind that came in through the broken window.

"We'll have to get another room," Fargo told her with a smile.

"I don't think there are any," she said.

"Then I'll get some boards and patch up that window so it won't be so cold in here."

She stood up and came into his arms as he closed the door behind him with his foot. "That's a good idea," she said, "but I can think of some other ways to help us keep warm, too."

Fargo brought his mouth down on hers as they kissed with a hungry, urgent passion. Victoria hadn't asked him about Mallory, and he wasn't going to tell her right away that the outlaw had vanished. There was no point in worrying her when Fargo was convinced that Mallory was either already dead or soon would be.

For the rest of tonight, he was going to do his level best to see that she put all of those bad memories behind her.

10

The captain of the riverboat was named Napier. The boat was called the *Tacoma,* even though they were quite a ways from Washington Territory. The grizzled old boatman had complained about finding room for the Ovaro, but in the end he agreed that Fargo could bring the stallion.

The *Tacoma* was scheduled to pull away from the dock at ten o'clock the next morning after Fargo's shootout with Smoky Jack Mallory. There had been no sign of the outlaw. Fargo made a brief visit behind the thick walls of the fort that morning and spoke with the commanding officer, telling him about the massacre at Fort Newcomb and asking him to have his patrols keep an eye out for Mallory's body.

"Hmmph," the captain said. "You'll never see that desperado again, Fargo. The wolves will take care of that."

Fargo didn't mention that one of the men in the saloon had said the same thing the night before. He just nodded and said, "Yes, sir, more than likely."

He returned to the Montana Belle and found Victoria ready to go. "Did you talk to the commanding officer at the fort?" she asked him.

Fargo nodded. "Captain Stennett extends his sympathies on behalf of the United States Army."

"Will they . . . will they send more men to Fort Newcomb?"

"I don't know," Fargo replied honestly. "Not until next spring, anyway, at the earliest. But the decision will be made in Washington, D.C., not out here."

"I'm not sure that we shouldn't just leave this land to the Indians," Victoria said, a trace of bitterness in her voice. Fargo couldn't blame her for feeling that way.

"Civilization's sort of like a big rock," he said. "Once you start it rolling down a hill, it's hard to stop."

Although, he added to himself, judging from many of the things he had seen in his eventful life, barbarism seemed more likely to be the natural state of mankind. . . .

The *Tacoma* chugged out into the river on schedule, water spraying high from the paddles on the big wheel at its stern. The boat was crowded. Some of the passengers would have to sleep out on deck at night, despite the cold. Fargo had managed to secure the last available cabin for himself and Victoria. There was no reason for them to spend the winter at Fort Benton if it wasn't necessary, and Victoria really wanted to return to her home in St. Louis. Fargo couldn't blame her for that.

Claiming exhaustion, she spent most of the day resting in the cabin. Fargo headed for the saloon deck, got himself a bottle, and soon found himself playing cards with a couple of fur trappers, an Army officer, and a pair of professional gamblers.

The tinhorns didn't realize it at first, but Fargo was just as good at cards as they were and could have made a living playing poker if he had so chosen. The game was straight, the professionals relying on their ability to bluff and read faces instead of cheating. They won the most, but nobody was cleaned out, and the atmosphere remained congenial. After the harrowing events he had encountered recently, the day was a very pleasant, relaxing one for Fargo.

When he went back to the cabin, Victoria said, "I don't really feel like going to the dining room to eat, Skye. Can't we have some food sent in here?"

He nodded and said, "I'll see what I can do," but something about Victoria's attitude was beginning to worry him. He had an idea what it was, too.

After they had eaten in the cabin, Fargo set the tray with the empty dishes outside on the deck for the steward to pick up. Then he went back in and opened a bottle of brandy he had brought with him from the saloon deck.

They each took a sip of the smooth, fiery liquor. Then Fargo said, "You know, there's no reason you have to hide out here in the cabin until we get back to St. Louis."

"H-hide?" she said. "What do you mean by that? I'm not hiding."

"You had a shawl around your head when you came on board, and you've been here in the cabin ever since."

"It was cold outside," she said sharply, a hint of the old defiance in her voice. "And I stayed in the cabin because I was tired."

"And you have every right to be, after what you've gone through," Fargo agreed. "But I'm wondering if that cut on your face has something to do with it, too."

His deliberately blunt statement made her raise her hand to her cheek. The cut was about two inches long, but it was clean and not too deep. Broken Hand's knife had been razor-sharp. The post surgeon had come to the Montana Belle that morning and stitched the wound closed. By the time the steamboat reached St. Louis, the injury would be healed, though Victoria would always have a narrow scar there as a reminder of what had happened.

"How can you say such a cruel thing, Skye?"

"I'm not trying to be cruel," Fargo said. "I just want you to realize that it doesn't matter."

"Doesn't matter?" she echoed. "Of course it matters! I . . . I've been mutilated—"

Fargo shook his head as he stepped closer to her and rested his hands on her shoulders. "You're still as beautiful a woman as I've ever seen," he said softly. "After last night, you should know that."

But he recalled now that although Victoria had made love with him passionately and eagerly, she had done so only after blowing out the lamp in the room on the second floor of the Montana Belle.

Now she tried to pull away from him, and when she couldn't do that, she turned her head so that he couldn't see her slashed cheek. "Please let me go," she said.

Normally, Fargo would have complied with that request. In this case, though, he didn't. He kept his left hand on her shoulder while he used his right to cup her chin and turn her face back toward him.

"That cut isn't who you are," he said. "The scar it'll leave behind isn't who you are. It's just one part—a very small part—of a beautiful, brave, intelligent woman." He smiled. "Maybe a mite too feisty for your own good sometimes, but that's all right, too."

"Skye, you do *not* understand. You can't understand. You're not a woman."

He moved his hand from her chin to her chest, just above her left breast. "I understand that it's what's inside a person that counts. I don't have to be a woman to know that."

He moved his hand lower, cupped her breast, and began to gently knead and caress it. She closed her eyes and sighed. Through her dress, he felt her nipple hardening.

Fargo leaned over and kissed her. He slid his tongue into her mouth, exploring all the hot, moist crannies of it as her tongue glided around his.

She leaned against him, molding her body to his. Fargo moved his left hand from her shoulder down to her hip. Her pelvis surged forward, grinding against the stiffening thrust of his manhood.

"Oh, Skye . . ." she whispered when Fargo broke the kiss.

Fargo trailed his lips over her nose and forehead, then stepped back. "Take your clothes off," he said.

"Oh, yes," she said, starting to turn away. "Let me get the lamp. . . ."

Fargo put out a hand to stop her. "Leave it burning. I want to see you. All of you."

"But . . ." She started to protest but then stopped. Giving him a slightly defiant look, she said, "Fine, if that's the way you want it."

"That's the way I want it," Fargo said with a nod.

Her hands went to the buttons of her dress. He noticed that her fingers trembled a little as she unfastened them. Without taking her eyes off his, she removed her dress and pushed down the shift underneath it, baring her breasts. Both large brown nipples were erect and stood out prominently.

"Don't read too much into that," she said when she saw him looking at them. "It's chilly in here."

"It is a mite chilly," Fargo agreed. "But we'll be under the blankets soon enough."

"That's what you think. Maybe I'll just give you a show and then send you packing."

"Maybe," Fargo said mildly, although he knew that was never going to happen.

Victoria continued undressing, her clothes going into a pile at her feet. When she finally stood nude before him, Fargo let his gaze rove slowly over her entire body, lingering on the triangle of dark brown hair between her legs, the bold thrust of her breasts, and then on her face, where he studied her brown eyes for what seemed like an eternity.

He moved toward her, taking his time about it, and leaned down to kiss her again. She tried not to respond at first, but her desire was too strong. She reached up and put her arms around Fargo's neck, drawing him closer to her.

His fingers combed through the finespun hair at the juncture of her thighs. Then his hand slipped between her legs and found her opening. The folds of flesh were already wet, and two fingers went into her easily. She gave a soft little cry and shuddered as he delved inside her.

"Oh . . . oh, Skye . . ." she whispered.

Fargo eased her back onto the bed. Her thighs parted instinctively, spreading wide, opening herself to him. Fargo had already hung up his hat and taken off his gun-belt. Now he went to his knees beside the bed and leaned forward between her legs. He showered kisses on her femininity, and then his tongue penetrated her.

Her hips bucked off the bed as a climax rippled through her. Fargo rode it out and continued, taking her from one height to the next with his lips and tongue. He was merciless in his passion, and he didn't stop until Victoria sagged back against the mattress, limp and breathless.

Fargo stood up and stripped off his buckskins. He slid onto the bed beside her and put his arms around her. When he rolled over, she had no choice but to go with him. She wound up lying on top of him, breasts flattened against his chest, his hands resting on the twin swells of her rump.

His shaft had grown long and thick and was so hard

it almost ached. He needed to be inside her, but he waited until she had caught her breath. Then he kissed her ear and whispered, "Sit up. I want you to ride me."

"The lamp . . ." she murmured.

"You know by now that nothing about you bothers me."

Victoria put her hands on his chest and pushed herself upright. Her legs parted again and her thighs slipped down on either side of his hips. His erect member thrust up between her legs, and as she scooted back a little, his sensitive flesh felt the heat of her core rubbing against it.

She moved her hips up and down, wetly caressing his manhood, and the motion excited both of them even more. She raised herself even higher and reached down to grasp his shaft and guide it into her. For a second, she poised there, with her opening resting on the head of his organ, and then she slid down it, taking it into herself.

Fargo's jaw tightened and he caught his breath as the exquisite sensation of penetrating her went through him. He reached up and used both hands to cup her breasts. He thumbed her nipples as she began to pump her hips.

She rode him just as he had asked, and he watched her face as she did it. He saw the excitement building in her eyes, saw the way her full red lips parted as she gasped for breath. She clutched at his chest, bracing herself as her bottom bounced up and down faster and faster. He knew it wouldn't be long before another climax seized her.

Fargo didn't want to wait, either. He matched her thrust for thrust. He was boiling now, ready to erupt into her.

His culmination rolled over him like an avalanche. He shuddered as he let himself go, driving up into her as deeply as he could. She cried out as yet another climax rippled through her.

She toppled forward onto his chest and lay there, rising and falling as he breathed deeply. He saw that her eyes were closed and her face had relaxed into a look of utter contentment. With a smile, Fargo reached down, got hold of the blankets, and pulled them up over both of them.

Later, when he was sure that Victoria was sound asleep, he slipped out of bed and blew out the lamp, plunging the cabin into darkness.

The Missouri River twisted and turned through the prairie landscape, usually between high clay bluffs. In the heat of summer, the level of the river always dropped so that numerous sandbars in the streambed posed a hazard to navigation. A riverboat captain had to be well aware of where those sandbars were located.

Several good rains during the fall had raised the water level, so staying in the deeper channels wasn't too difficult. The *Tacoma* maintained a good head of steam and traveled downriver at a good pace. It would still take several weeks to reach St. Louis, but Fargo didn't mind. He had good company in Victoria.

However, he wasn't sure he would remain in St. Louis when the riverboat got there. Victoria still had family in the city. They would welcome her and see that she got back on her feet.

Winter was blowing in up here in the Montana country, but farther south, say in Texas or Louisiana or New Mexico Territory, the weather wouldn't be too bad for a while yet. By the time they reached St. Louis, the Ovaro would be ready to stretch his legs. Fargo thought he just might oblige the stallion.

He decided not to say anything about that to Victoria just yet. He thought she would accept his decision without any weeping and wailing; she was a strong woman, no doubt about that. But for now he was content to laze away the days and nights without borrowing trouble.

The weather even cooperated. The skies cleared, and the temperatures rose; it was almost warm again for a couple of days. Fargo knew the respite wouldn't last long, and when winter returned it would likely come back with a vengeance, with howling winds, blinding blizzards, and cold so intense that eventually a sheet of ice would form over the river itself, making travel by boat impossible until the spring.

Captain Napier guided the boat close to the north bank of the river and brought it to a stop there. Fargo was standing on-deck at the time and saw several of the deckhands go ashore carrying axes. He was high enough that he could see some scrubby trees about a quarter of a mile away. Trees were few and far between out here on the prairie, so Napier was taking this opportunity to replenish his wood boxes. That was the prudent thing to do.

Victoria came up behind Fargo and asked, "Skye, why are we stopping in the middle of the afternoon?"

Fargo pointed to the woodcutting party. "They're going to go chop down some of those trees. We have to have wood to burn to keep up the steam."

"Could we go ashore, too? I'd love to get off this boat and stretch my legs for a while."

That sounded like a pretty good idea to Fargo, too. Some of the other travelers were already doing just that, jumping from the deck to a narrow sand beach at the edge of the river, then climbing a trail on the bank up to the prairie.

Fargo smiled and took Victoria's hand. "Sure, let's go."

A few minutes later they reached the top of the bank and looked out across the gently rolling plains.

The snow had melted, exposing brown, dead grass that rustled as the wind blew across it. Not really what anybody would call a pretty picture, Fargo thought, but the scene had a certain stark appeal to it. No matter what the season, it was difficult not to see the grandeur of this vast, empty land.

Victoria began walking. Fargo strolled along with her. They talked of inconsequential things—it was nice to be able to do that after the dangers they had shared together. Victoria headed up a long, shallow rise. When she and Fargo reached the top of it, they were close to half a mile from the river, Fargo estimated. Looking back in that direction, they could see the trees where the woodcutters still worked, the sound of their axes biting into tree trunks carrying easily in the clear air.

In the other direction, the prairie swept away for mile after untold mile, until finally, far in the distance, snow-capped mountains rose. Victoria pointed at them and asked, "Are those in Canada?"

"Nope, those are the Bear Paws," Fargo said. "Believe it or not, the border is a good long ways on the other side of those mountains. It's a long way to anywhere, up here in this country."

She smiled over at him. "Are you sure we shouldn't just leave it for the Indians?"

"You've got me convinced," he told her. "Now if you can just persuade the politicians in Washington. . . ."

She laughed and leaned against him, resting her head on his shoulder.

Fargo was so relaxed and content at that moment that he didn't hear the rush of footsteps in the grass until it was almost too late.

He whirled and shoved Victoria away from him with his left hand while his right dipped to the holster on his hip and palmed out the Colt. A gun roared, and Fargo heard the wind-rip of a bullet as it sizzled through the air between him and Victoria. He fired at the wild-eyed, shaggy shape charging him, and the roar of the Colt blended with the second shot fired by the attacker.

What felt like a giant fist slammed into Fargo's shoulder, numbing his right arm all the way to the tips of his fingers. The Colt started to slip from his grasp. He reached over with his left hand and grabbed it, but before he could bring it into play again, the man crashed into him and knocked him over backwards.

He had caught just a glimpse of the man's face in the tangle of beard and long hair, but he recognized his attacker. For an instant, the thought that Smoky Jack Mallory had come back from the grave filled Fargo's brain with horror, but then he realized that, somehow, Mallory was alive.

Very much alive, and trying to kill him, in fact.

Fargo got his left hand on Mallory's coat and heaved to the side as he arched his back from the ground. Mallory tumbled away, rolling a couple of times. The collision had caused Fargo to drop the revolver. He looked around for it as he came up on his hands and knees. He still couldn't use his right arm and hand, but he could shoot well enough left-handed, given the chance.

Mallory didn't intend to give him that chance. The outlaw came up in a crouch and thrust the barrel of a Henry rifle at Fargo. "Hold it!" he yelled.

Fargo had just spotted the Colt lying in the short grass about four feet away from him. If he lunged for the weapon, though, Mallory would fire, and at this range the outlaw could hardly miss. Fargo froze, only his eyes moving as he looked for Victoria.

He saw her about fifteen feet to his right, staring at Mallory in horrified disbelief. "You . . . you're dead!" she said.

He leered at her. "Nope. Maybe I should be, but I

ain't." To Fargo, he went on. "You done your best to kill me, you son of a bitch. Shot me four times, all told. But I'm still breathin'."

"You must've had help," Fargo said. He heard shouts from the woodcutting party and knew they would be coming to investigate the shots. If he could just stall for a few minutes . . . "Otherwise you would have died when you rode off from Fort Benton."

"Sure, I was a goner," Mallory agreed. "But a few miles out of town, I ran into a couple of trappers on their way to spend the winter at the fort. They had a nice outfit and a fair amount of supplies. Plenty for me after I killed both of 'em. I waited until they'd patched up my bullet holes, though, before I did it."

"I can guess the rest," Fargo said. "You slipped back into Fort Benton, found out we'd left on the riverboat, and you've been following us, just waiting for a chance to jump us. And we gave you that chance today."

"You sure did. Why do you reckon I did all that, Fargo? What's been keepin' me alive when by all rights I oughta be dead?"

"Hate," Fargo said. "Pure, crazy hate."

"Damn right. Now I'm gonna kill you and the girl's comin' with me, just like it was supposed to be all along." The Henry rifle came up as Mallory got ready to fire. "See you in hell, Fargo."

The sharp crack of a gunshot came from Fargo's right. Mallory jerked at the impact of a bullet as he squeezed the rifle's trigger. The Henry roared, but the shot went wild. At the same instant, Fargo dived toward his Colt and came up with the revolver in his left hand. He fired again and again.

The slugs thudded into Mallory's body and drove him backwards in a grisly dance. There was no window for him to fall out of this time, so Fargo was able to empty the Colt into him. Mallory dropped the rifle and finally came to a stop. He swayed back and forth and stared down at his bullet-riddled torso. He looked up at Fargo and said, "You . . ."

That was all he got out before he toppled over, dead by the time he hit the ground.

Fargo got to his feet and looked over at Victoria. She still had her right arm extended stiffly in front of her, a small pistol clutched tightly in her hand. Fargo didn't know where the gun had come from, but right now that didn't matter.

"It's over," he said. "Mallory's dead."

Victoria swallowed. "No offense, Skye, but I've heard that before. Would you mind checking?"

Some of the numbness had worn off in Fargo's right hand, enabling him to use it to help reload the Colt. Then he strode over to Mallory's body and looked down into the wide, staring, glassy eyes.

"He's dead. No doubt about it this time."

Victoria released the breath she had been holding in a long sigh. She lowered the gun and slipped it back into the pocket of her coat.

"I bought the gun from one of the bartenders at the Montana Belle," she said as she looked at Fargo. "While you were up at the fort talking to the commanding officer. I didn't ever want to be without a way to defend myself again. Maybe . . . maybe even then I was afraid that Mallory wasn't really dead."

"It's a good thing you felt that way," Fargo said as he holstered the Colt. Mallory's bullet had just grazed his shoulder. As he moved it around, he could tell that no real damage had been done. The arm and shoulder would be stiff and sore for a while, but that was all.

And right now it worked just fine for pulling Victoria into an embrace and holding her against him as the woodcutters charged up the hill. Down below on the river, a blast of steam came from the *Tacoma*'s stack in a shrill whistle. The sound pulled at something inside him.

He was ready to put this wild Montana country and all its killing behind him for a while, but sooner or later it would call him back.

The frontier always did.

LOOKING FORWARD!
The following is the opening section of the next novel in the exciting *Trailsman* series from Signet:

THE TRAILSMAN #274

Nebraska Nightmare

Nebraska, 1860—
Let he who stands without sin cast the first stone,
let he who fires the first shot fire true—
for when the Trailsman comes to town,
final judgment arrives with better aim than most.

If Skye Fargo had learned one thing in all his travels, it was that trouble waited for you in the most unexpected places.

Take tonight. A pleasant early October evening near the town of Gladville, Nebraska. The smoky smell of autumn in the timberland surrounding the valley. Fargo wanted a real bath and a real bed for the simple reason that he'd gone too long without them. He was coming off the tail end of a cattle drive that had not gone well, thanks to a power-mad cattle baron who had been under the mistaken impression that hired hands were his personal slaves.

Peace and quiet tonight and then some whiskey, women and song tomorrow. He'd always heard that Gladville was a wide-open town.

As he came down the steep, rocky hill that led to the trail that would eventually take him to the town, he saw what he first thought was a bundle of rags glowing white in the moonlight. Something dropped accidentally from a Conestoga, maybe. Or somebody just throwing some old clothes away.

The rags lay next to the trail, so he had to pass them on his way into town. He took notice when the rags rolled over with no help from the windless night. Rags didn't just roll over of their own accord, now did they?

He dropped from his big Ovaro stallion, jerked his Colt from its holster and moved closer for a look-see.

A young woman. But he couldn't see much; her still-pretty face had been beaten on with considerable force.

He eased up to her. This could always be some kind of trap. Somebody hiding in the nearby timber with the girl as a lure. The facial bruises applied with dirt.

His gaze roamed the timber around him. He searched for any sign of another human being. He listened for sounds, too. But there was nothing to indicate that anybody else was around.

He went back to his stallion and grabbed his canteen. When he had raised the girl up sufficiently, he tipped the mouth of the canteen to her lips. Her blue eyes fluttered open. Her shriek was so unexpected that he damn near dropped both the canteen and the girl.

She struggled to get away, but the gouge in the back of her head sapped her strength.

"Calm down," he said gently. "I'm going to help you. But you have to help me, too. You need water and then you need a doc."

Every few moments, her entire body would jerk with pain. Then she raised a hand as if in entreaty, and fell back in his grasp. She was unconscious—or dead.

Fargo had the eerie sense he was entering a ghost town. A place named Gladville should greet visitors with the open arms of harlots and open bottles of good whiskey.

Here and there on either side of the trail he saw a light or two in one of the tiny huddled houses that made up the residential parts of the place. But the business area was dark and silent in a way that was almost sullen. None of the places that advertised themselves as saloons were open.

He was looking for a doctor's sign anywhere. With her wounds, the girl needed medical attention immediately. It took him several long minutes to find one. There, down near the river that ran from east to west, he found a yard sign that said MEDICAL DOCTOR. A small white house with a picket fence; a nice new buggy next to a shanty that housed it; and a single horse. No lights. But Fargo wasn't discouraged. No lights simply meant that the doc was probably getting some well-deserved sleep.

By this time, the girl was delirious. She moaned and wailed like a creature of the supernatural as she lay against the tree where Fargo had propped her up.

Fargo opened the gate in the picket fence and went up to the door of the house. He knocked loudly enough to be heard but not so loud as to irritate the doc. He had to knock several times before he got any response. And the response he got was neither what he wanted or expected.

Instead of coming to the door, a short man in a nightshirt carried a small lantern to the front window and peeked out at Fargo. A nimbus of white hair gave him a fatherly look his crabbed facial features belied.

"Who are you?" the elderly doctor demanded in a squeaky voice.

"Who are *you*?" Fargo demanded back.

"Doc Mathers."

"My name's Fargo. Got a girl here who's dying. She needs help bad."

"Who is she?"

"I don't know—and what the hell's the difference? She needs a doc."

The old man cursed but he came out onto the small wooden slab of porch. He was barefooted. Fargo had spread his blanket on the ground and settled the girl on top of it.

The doc followed Fargo over to the insensate woman, held his lantern down to her face and said, "Holy hell."

"What?"

"I can't help you, feller."

"Why the hell not?"

"Because the Sister put the word out on her. Nobody's s'posed to help her."

"I don't give a damn. This girl needs help and you're going to give it to her. You're a doc."

"Don't docs have a right to refuse patients?"

"Not this doc and not this girl."

Then both doc and lantern disappeared, leaving

Fargo confused and angry. What kind of doc would turn away a dying patient? And why had he declined to offer his services only after he saw the girl?

This time, Fargo pounded on the door with both fists. Each time he paused, he could hear the girl wailing again in that ghostly voice of hers.

He then took to shouting. "I don't want to bust open this door, Doc, but I will if you don't come out here right now."

He tried this three times—sounding like the big bad wolf—and then backed up several yards and canted just to the right so that his shoulder would hit the door just above the knob, popping it open.

He was ready to storm the door when a shotgun blast opened up a huge hole in the middle of the pine slab. "You get out of here, mister!" yelled the doc. "I give you any help at all, the Sister'll burn my house down. Now you take that girl and get the hell out of here."

Who the hell was this "Sister"? And why would anybody kill the doc for doing his duty? What the hell was going on in this town? First the saloons being closed up tight way before midnight. And now a doc who refused to help a dying girl because he was afraid somebody would kill him.

The girl had started wailing again and it unnerved Fargo. He felt so helpless. She was going to slip into death and there wasn't a damn thing he could do about it. Only the little old man inside could help her. And he didn't have long to do it.

Fargo decided that he could probably fake the old doc out. He crept around to the back of the house. The horse that was bedded down in the shanty for the night made all the noise Fargo had hoped. Wake a horse in the middle of the night and he's likely to do some complaining. The doc—unless he was stone deaf—was likely to hear it, which was exactly what Fargo wanted.

Fargo began pelting the back door with the heaviest rocks he could find. The doc responded with more buckshot, putting the same size holes in the back door as he had in the front. Fargo knew he had to be patient to keep up this ruse. He continued to pelt the back wall and the back door with anything he could find. The doc switched to some kind of handgun. Neither the bark of the gun nor the holes in the door were so dramatic anymore but the old fart kept at it.

Once he believed that he'd convinced the doc that he was trying to get in the back way, Fargo hurried around front and took the chance of smashing in the door with his shoulder as he'd originally planned.

He stood several yards from the door, put his head down, scraped his boots against the patch of earth that led to the house and charged.

First thing: the door was a hell of a lot more formidable than Fargo had estimated. Or maybe it was just the way he hit it. Either way, he was going to have one hell of a bruise on that shoulder in short order.

Second thing: the old doc *was* on to his plan. He'd taken up his shotgun again and started blasting away the moment he heard Fargo's shoulder hit the door.

Third thing: because the door was collapsing inward just as he was firing, the doc's shots missed Fargo by two feet.

Fargo, angry, confused and needing very badly to put some hurt on this old bastard, did not slow down when he got inside the house. He drove straight for the old man, grabbing him around the middle and dragging him all the way back into a table topped with many small porcelain figures that went flying, smashing against each other in midair, breaking against the wall, shattering as they hit the floor.

The doc's shotgun went flying, too. Fargo jumped to his feet and grabbed him by the front of his nightshirt. "Now you're going to help that girl, Doc, or you're going to find yourself worse off than she is now."

He jammed the barrel of his Colt against the doc's wrinkled neck to make his point.

Fargo couldn't be absolutely sure, but he had the impression that the doc had just wet himself.

While the doc worked on the woman in his back office, Fargo slept on the floor in the front room. He was a light sleeper. His Colt was on his stomach. He'd hear the doc coming and he'd be ready.

A ticking clock was the first sound he was aware of when he woke—a small decorative clock on the living room mantel. It was nearly seven in the morning.

He was on his feet, then he rushed to the other room where he found a rolltop desk and a bookcase filled with medical tomes. The doc had his head down on the writing surface of the desk. He was snoring. But he must have been a light sleeper, too; he jerked awake before Fargo was even three steps into the office.

"She's on my table in there," the doc said. "She's dead." He looked up at Fargo with an almost childlike terror in his eyes. "And now thanks to you that damned Sister's gonna come after me. Her and her gunnies."

"What're you talking about?" Fargo demanded.

"Go to that front window and take a look outside."

The odd way the old doc was carrying on, Fargo expected him to say there were ghosts waiting out there. Fargo decided to have a look, anyway. Humor the old guy.

He went to the window and slipped back the curtain. At first, he thought he was seeing an optical illusion. The three people wore capes and cowls, like monks. Their attire was so dark, it fitted into the night seamlessly, so that they seemed to be one with the darkness itself. They were spooky enough to raise Fargo's hackles.

"Who're they?"

"You stay in this town long enough, you'll find out. And they sure ain't gonna like it that you brought her here. I took care of one of the people they worked over and the next night while I was out on a call, somebody broke in here and destroyed my place. I don't want to tangle with them folks again. They sure hated that girl you brought in."

"Why?"

"Because she and her sister stood up to them."

"You think they did this to the girl?"

"I ain't sayin'. It's none of my business. And you can't make me say it." The old doc sounded like he was about five years old. He was terrified.

Fargo watched the three figures as they in turn watched him. Their faces were lost in the folds and shadows of their cowls. He couldn't even be sure of their gender. Just three dark figures standing there watching.

"Maybe I'll go talk to 'em."

"Won't do you no good. They won't talk to you. Not them. They's special. Them that wear those hoods. They're like them priests that take the vow of silence. Won't say a word to nobody."

Fargo had the sense that he'd stepped inside a bad dream. "Where's the law in all this?"

The old doc snorted. "The law? That's somethin' else you'll need to find out for yourself."

"There's a sheriff, isn't there?"

"There's a feller that wears a badge, if that's what you mean. Used to be the finest lawman I ever knew. But not no more."

Fargo let the curtain fall back in place. Then he went and got the girl and carried her outside to his stallion. He kept her wrapped warm in his blanket. He knew she was dead, but keeping her warm was just something he wanted to do. The three cowled figures watched silently.